Julie smiled as she cruised toward the highway. The speed and the wind and the music made her feel alive and free. She knew that she didn't have too many more weeks of this kind of freedom.

She pulled into the left lane to pass the slow-moving flatbed truck in front of her. Up ahead, the highway curved sharply.

Slow down, Julie told herself. *Precious cargo on board.* She put one hand on her pregnant stomach as she pressed the brake with her right foot. She heard a shrill squeak, then the brake pedal collapsed to the floor. The car didn't slow down.

Julie felt her body tighten with fear. She pushed down on the brake again. Nothing happened. The car was sailing full speed toward the curve in the road. She yanked the steering wheel to the right. The car lurched with the abrupt movement.

Terror rose in Julie's chest. The metal lane divider loomed up right in front of her eyes. *"No!"*

Julie pressed her hands over the baby. *My baby and me. We're going to die.*

Don't miss the other books
in this romantic series, **First Comes Love:**

To Have and to Hold
For Better, for Worse
In Sickness and in Health

TILL DEATH DO US PART

Jennifer Baker

SCHOLASTIC INC.
New York Toronto London Auckland Sydney

ISBN 0-590-46316-0

Copyright © 1993 by Daniel Weiss Associates, Inc., and Jennifer Baker. All rights reserved. Published by Scholastic Inc.

Produced by Daniel Weiss Associates, Inc.
33 West 17th Street, New York, NY 10011

12 11 10 9 8 7 6 5 4 3 2 1   3 4 5 6 7 8/9

Printed in the U.S.A.   01

First Scholastic printing, August 1993

One

❧

"This one's my favorite." Julie Miller-Collins pointed to a fluffy comforter. "I love the ducks and geese."

"Figures," Matt Collins said. "I don't suppose it has anything to do with the fact that they're *pink* ducks and geese?"

Julie laughed and rolled her eyes. "Wow, and I thought I was married to a modern guy. You know, it's not illegal to have a little pink on something for a baby boy," she said. She and Matt ambled down the aisle past the row of model nurseries set up side by side to display some of Baby World's merchandise. "Besides, I don't know how you can be so sure that it's not going to be a girl—like my intuition tells me."

She stopped walking and put her hands on her full, round belly. Six months into her preg-

1

nancy, she felt a current of joy and amazement at what was happening in her body. A tiny new life was forming, a human being made from her and Matt's love.

Matt covered Julie's hands with his own. "Well, we'll see who's right, won't we?" He leaned forward, and his lips brushed hers lightly. Julie gave a shiver of happiness. Boy, girl—it didn't matter one bit.

She smiled up at Matt, caressing his face with her gaze—his deep-set gray eyes, full lips with a freckle near the side of his mouth, straight, broad nose. His dark hair had grown in as thick and shiny as ever now that his terrifying struggle against Hodgkin's disease had been won. Julie felt a crashing wave of relief that the nightmare of almost losing him was behind her. He still had to go for checkups once a month, but his doctor felt confident that his cancer was nearing complete and permanent remission.

Matt certainly looked healthy, Julie thought. Wait. Scratch that. He *was* healthy, she told herself—healthy and handsome. In his T-shirt and faded jeans, he didn't look too different than he had back in high school, when they'd first fallen in love. But now he was going to be a father—the father of her baby! A tremor of amazement went through her.

Matt smiled back at her. "What is it?" he asked, his hands still cradling hers over her belly.

Julie shook her head. "I still just can't believe it, sometimes," she said. "Us—parents. I mean, Matt, do you realize that this time last year I was getting ready for college and we were getting ready to say good-bye?"

Julie remembered being upstairs in her bedroom in Philadelphia, packing for her first year at Madison College, tears streaming down her face at the thought of going off to Ohio and leaving Matt behind.

"Yeah, I don't know how I ever thought I was going to be able to let you go for four years," Matt said.

"I *knew* I couldn't do it," Julie said. She'd never forget a second of their reunion as long as she lived—waking up in the middle of the night to Matt's kiss as she lay in her bed in her dorm room, holding him, not quite being able to believe he was real. Making love for the first time, heady with tenderness and intimacy, feeling her soul open to Matt's. Falling asleep in his arms. And the next day—racing to the Maryland border on Matt's motorcycle, exchanging marriage vows in a tiny, sunny town hall. "Yeah, a lot has happened in a year. It does seem kind of amazing. We got married, I got sick . . ."

"And well again," Julie put in quickly. "And now—we're about to be parents!" she added. The baby hadn't been something she and Matt had planned. Far from it. But once they'd weighed the possibilities, they'd discovered just how much they wanted the little creature growing inside Julie. And they were both sure that this new life had played a part in Matt's speedy recovery from his illness.

"About to be parents and we can't even decide on a comforter," Matt joked. "Or a crib to put it in, for that matter." He took his hands from Julie's stomach and turned back to the display of cribs and bedding. "I don't know. What about this plain wooden crib over here? It's nice and simple. It's—"

"Not pink?" Julie teased.

"That's not what I was going to say," Matt protested.

"Can I help you folks with something?" a deep voice boomed. Julie turned to see a sandy-haired salesman, not much older than she and Matt. The name RANDY was printed on his Baby World name tag.

Matt laughed. "Yeah. We need a crib, a stroller, a changing table, about a zillion diapers—let's see, what am I leaving out? Oh, yeah, a name for the baby. Any suggestions? We can't seem to decide on anything."

Randy laughed, too. "Hey, I know you, don't I?" he said. "You're the guy who does Club Night over at the Barn and Grill."

Matt grinned. "Guilty as charged. I also wait tables there and do whatever else needs to be done."

"Yeah, I thought I recognized you. Well, Club Night's totally cool. We needed something like that around here," Randy said. "Good music, a place to dance. I caught that show you put on out on the Town Green, too. The one with all those bands. It was hot! Hey, you know, my cousin's got a band—Lunar Eclipse. They're really good."

Julie smiled to herself. *Married to a celebrity,* she thought. Back when Matt had first come out to Ohio, he'd been sure he'd never feel at home in Madison. Now it was impossible to go anywhere without having someone come up and talk music with him, or tell him how his brother played guitar, or his niece was a singer, and did Matt think he could get them a gig?

"Your cousin should drop off a demo tape at the Barn and Grill," Matt said. "I'm always listening to new stuff. Now, about the crib and all those diapers . . ."

"Oh, yeah," Randy said. "Cribs. Strollers. Can't make up your minds. Well, you've got a little time, don't you?" He glanced at Julie's belly.

Julie felt herself blush. "Three more months," she said. "The baby's due in late November."

"So you don't have to decide everything right away."

"Well, actually, we wanted to get as much of the nursery furnished as we could before school starts," Julie explained. "I mean, the baby's due before the end of the semester, so I'm going to have to take some incompletes, but I need to stay as on top of my schoolwork as possible—get as much done as I can before the baby's born." She found herself reminding herself as much as explaining to the salesman.

"Plus, she has a job at the *Register*," Matt said. Julie could hear the note of pride in his voice over what had been initially only a summer job. Julie's boss had liked her work so much, she'd made her a permanent, part-time reporter. Okay, so maybe they did assign her articles about the Madison police force's end-of-summer barbecue, or the mysterious smell coming from the back of the Dress Shop. It wasn't ground-breaking journalism. And most of the time, Julie was answering phones or doing computer work at the newspaper's office. But Matt seemed to think *she* was the town celebrity.

"Anyway, we're both so busy," Matt was saying. "We're reopening the Barn and Grill after doing some renovations, and then I'm going to be taking a business course during the college fall semester, too."

Randy whistled through his teeth. "Pretty busy. I'll say."

"Yeah," Matt said. Julie noted the edge of excitement in his voice. It was the same tone he used to plan a winter camping trip, a long-distance run, or a day of white-water rafting. She was thrilled that Matt was able to enjoy life again now that the shadow of his illness was gone, and that the baby was as much of an adventure as anything he could imagine. He was about to be a father! And she was going to be a mother!

As if on cue, Julie felt the baby give a kick. She let out a little gasp of laughter. "She's kicking. I think she's trying to tell us something: Mommy, Daddy, get to work on my room."

Matt moved his hand back to Julie's stomach. "Hey, yeah! There *he* goes again." He winked at Julie.

"She's definitely trying to tell us that she likes the comforter with the pink ducks and geese," Julie said.

The morning sunlight filtered into the tent.

Dahlia Sussman snuggled closer to Nicholas Stone in the two sleeping bags they'd zipped together. "You up?" she whispered, peering at him through sleepy eyes.

"Hmm?" Nick buried his head under the sweater he'd been using as a pillow.

Dahlia pushed the sweater away. "Are you awake?" She showered him with kisses on his cheeks, his closed eyelids, his brow.

Nick rolled over on his back and opened one green eye. "I am now," he said in a throaty voice. "Since when are you the big early bird?"

Dahlia traced the outlines of Nick's fine-featured face with her fingers and ran her hand through his light-brown hair. "Since it's the last day of our trip." She let out a sigh. "I wish we had another two weeks."

Nick pushed up on one elbow. "Me, too. I wish we had time to hike in that canyon north of Santa Fe again."

"Yeah, and we could stop at that trading post. The one where I got those Navajo earrings? I wish I'd gotten the bracelet to match."

"Shop till you drop?" Nick teased.

Dahlia pouted.

"Hey, it's okay," Nick said. "I mean, you can take the girl out of New York City, but you can't take New York City out of the girl."

"Nick, that's not fair," Dahlia said. "I mean,

I've hiked just as many miles as you on this trip, and cooked just as many meals on that butane stove—okay, almost as many. And pitched the tent and . . . gone without my hair dryer for two weeks." She giggled. "Not only that, I've had a totally great time." She kissed Nick lightly on the lips. He responded, drawing her in closer for a longer, deeper kiss. His lips were warm, and she could feel his body against hers.

"Mmmm. Maybe we can just be a little late getting back to school," Dahlia murmured. "Or not go back at all. Now, there's an idea."

Nick kissed her again. "Hey, it's not like we're going to be separated once we get there, roomie."

Roomie. Roommate. Dahlia felt a sizzle of excitement—and a sting of fear. Officially, Nick was going to be rooming with Paul Chase, Dahlia's old pal from New York. And Dahlia had signed up to room with Paul's girlfriend, Maya. But that was only the version that went on record. Back at the end of freshman year, before summer vacation, Paul had suggested a kind of roommate swap. "You know, the old boy-girl, boy-girl thing," he'd said in his half-cool, half-goofy way.

The roommate-exchange program was what the four of them had unofficially called it. A little voice in the back of Dahlia's head had told her to slow down. Caution, proceed with care. One step at a time. It had taken all year to get Nick to fall for her, and she didn't want to risk messing up what they had. But things were so great between them, and Nick was so special, she didn't want to hold back, either. The idea of beginning and ending every day with him was irresistible. And Dahlia had never been very successful at saying no to what she really wanted.

So it had been decided. Nick and Dahlia would be moving into the room in West Hall. Paul and Maya would get the room in Manning House. And Dahlia just had to pray her parents wouldn't find out.

"Dahlia? You okay?" Nick asked, stroking her long blond hair.

"Huh? Oh, yeah. I was just thinking about my folks. They'll kill me if they find out." Even now, they thought Dahlia was camping out with a bunch of friends from Madison. "Or cut off my checking account. Again. I don't know which is worse," Dahlia cracked. "Can you imagine? One of *the* Sussmans of *the* Sussmans' clothing empire, a total pauper."

Nick frowned. "Dahlia, why are you so sure your parents won't understand? It's not like they're so strict or anything. And I mean, mine weren't exactly dancing on the tables or anything, but they know I really love you, and they're trying to respect my decision."

Dahlia felt a shiver of pleasure at Nick's words. *I love you.* For so long, she'd only dreamed of his feeling that way. It had taken almost the whole year to get past their disastrous ride home from school over last Thanksgiving vacation. It had been nearly a year ago, but she remembered it clearly.

"Why not?" Dahlia had said when Julie asked if she could give her friend Nick a ride to New York City. Totally cute guy, fun drive, good tunes on the tape deck. But her car had broken down in a blizzard halfway home, and things had gone completely downhill from there. Nick had spent most of freshman year thinking Dahlia was a spoiled brat. And Dahlia had spent most of the year trying to forget about Nick—but finding herself hopelessly stuck on the guy. Second semester, she'd even taken an upper-level art history course on the Sistine Chapel in Rome—a class that she was unprepared for—just so she could sit next to him three times a week.

And miracle of miracles, Nick had finally started to come around. Dahlia had even managed to ace a course for the first time, too. Of course, it had helped that she'd been to Rome and seen the Sistine Chapel three times. But she'd worked harder than she ever had in that

11

class—both on the assignments and on Nick. And here they were sharing a tent, the magic of the great plains and mesas of the Southwest all around them. When Nick had finally fallen, he'd fallen hard. Still, it didn't make her nervousness about their new living arrangements or her parents go away.

"Look, Nick, it's not the boy-girl thing. That's not it. I mean, I think my folks got pretty used to my having boyfriends in high school."

A flicker of jealousy crossed Nick's face. "High school, Nick." Dahlia laughed. But the laugh faded. "The thing is, Mother and Daddy are pretty ticked off that my grades weren't better last year, and they pretty much blame my social life. See, you have a real family," she said. "Mine—sometimes I think it's just another one of Daddy's business arrangements. Send Dahlia to college, buy her a car, give her a bunch of charge cards. I call home once in a while, go back and do the holiday thing with them on school vacations, and voilà! They've bought themselves a real, live college daughter who they can talk about at dinner parties. As long as she doesn't embarrass them by flunking out." Dahlia's voice rose to the top of the cozy little tent.

Nick wound his arms around her and kissed her forehead softly. "Hey, I didn't mean to get you all worked up. I just think that it takes both

12

sides to try and communicate a little. Maybe if you really tried to talk to your parents, they'd listen a little harder."

Dahlia's body felt tense. "And maybe they wouldn't. When I fessed up about secretly paying Julie's tuition, they had a total fit. 'Oh, so you decided to play fairy godmother to one of your little friends,'" Dahlia said, imitating her mother's high-pitched voice. "She barely listened when I explained that Julie and Matt had insisted on paying me back."

"Dahlia, you can't blame your folks for kind of freaking out when they found out that a pretty giant chunk of money was missing from your bank account."

Dahlia laughed grimly. "Yeah. Drugs. That's what they thought. If they spent any time with me at all, they'd know that wasn't the problem. I guess they believed me, because they unfroze my bank account, but they were still furious about my grades and my social life and the money I gave Julie—everything they could think of." Dahlia let out a long breath.

"But what was I supposed to do about Julie?" She frowned. "I mean, after she and Matt eloped and her parents told her she was on her own . . . well, I didn't want her to have to drop out of school. And I knew she wouldn't take the money from me if I came right out and offered it to her. And then when Matt got sick, and they had all those bills to pay . . . Listen, the money was just sitting in the bank, not doing anything for anybody! So I wrote a few checks on the sly, paid a few expenses."

Nick laughed. "A few major expenses. But, Dahlia, you don't have to convince me. I think I started realizing I had the wrong idea about you when I saw how incredibly loyal you are to your friends."

She gave him a kiss on the forehead. "Thanks. You're sweet. But you know that's exactly what my parents think is a problem. 'We're sending you to college to get an education, not to revolve your life around your friends like you did all through high school.' That's really why they'd hit the ceiling if they knew about us living together." Dahlia ran her hands through her hair nervously. "You know—they think it means they're not getting the right return on their investment or something." She sighed. "Anyway, I don't want to spoil our last day of vacation talking about Mother and Daddy."

Dahlia sat up and found her sweatpants and T-shirt beside the sleeping bag. She pulled her T-shirt over her head. "One thing I won't mind about getting back to school is having some clean clothes and a hot shower in the morning," she said.

Nick laughed. "Yeah, I admit it—I can relate. Plus it'll be good to see people again. Catch up on everyone's summers and stuff. Especially our favorite Mom- and Dad-to-be." Nick wriggled into his cutoffs.

"Yeah, when I called Julie from New York a few weeks ago, she said she was getting really huge. I still can't believe those guys are going to have a baby! Jeez, I remember when I first got to Madison and Julie was my roommate. I couldn't believe she was spending so much time mooning over some guy who was four hundred miles away. And now they're going to be parents!"

Dahlia opened the tent flap and stepped outside. From the mesa-top plateau of the campsite, the huge, mitten-shaped red rock formations of Monument Valley rose up out of the desert floor in the distance. Other strange-shaped masses of rock dotted the landscape like some eerie sculpture garden. The sky was blue-white and vast. The air was still cool and slightly dusty.

Nick stepped out beside her. Dahlia could feel him right behind her, taking in the awesome scenery. "Wow, is it spectacular. Kind of weird to think that in three days we're going to be back in pancake-flat old Ohio."

"If we don't break down again like we did once upon a time," Dahlia joked. "I mean, my

15

brakes *have* been sounding kind of squeaky."

Nick gave her a fake punch on the shoulder. "Don't even say it. Now, how about if we whip up some yummy campfire gruel and go see about renting some horses for a last ride?"

Dahlia gazed out across the desert. She could almost feel the hooves beating beneath her as she galloped past the giant red rocks, the breeze on her face, Nick beside her. "Perfect end to a perfect vacation."

Two

❧

Matt sat at the newly refinished bar of the Barn and Grill with his bosses, Jake and Pat Howard. They all had their eyes glued to the front door to see who their first customer would be.

Matt broke into a wide grin as he saw Marcy, the regular of regulars, walk through the door. "As expected," he said. "She was the last one to leave when we closed for the renovation and she's the first one back for the opening."

"Okay, you win." Jake laughed as he reached into his pocket and pulled out a quarter.

"Nah, forget the bet," Matt said. "Too much like taking candy from a baby."

Dressed in faded blue denim from head to toe, Marcy smiled and gave them all a big wave. "How's it going?"

"Hi, Marcy," Pat said. "Welcome back."

"Finally! I thought you guys would never re-open," she said, making her way to her regular table and plopping down in a wooden chair. The door opened again, and a few of Marcy's friends came in to join her.

Jake got down off his bar stool and went over to the table. "So, what do you think, everyone?" He gestured around the restaurant to point out the work that had been done. "Not bad, huh?"

Matt didn't have to hear a response to know that they all approved. Marcy's eyes were wide with excitement as she took in all the changes. "Nice," she said, exclaiming over an entire new room just off the main space. Matt, Jake, and Pat had spent a good deal of the summer building the addition.

"We're going to move the tables and chairs out of that room on Friday for Club Night," Matt told her. "There'll be enough room for the whole state to dance."

"And hey, whoa, check it out," Marcy said to her friends as she gazed up at the hayloft at the front of the restaurant. "We've gone big time!"

They'd extended the hayloft out a few feet to make the stage larger. The ceiling overhead had been raised, too, so that they could fit in stage lights and better sound equipment. The lamps and speakers hung there now, as if waiting for Friday night to roll around.

"Burgers on the house for all you guys," Pat said as she headed toward the kitchen. She tucked her hair into her big white chef's hat. "Jake, I bet our favorite customers are thirsty."

"Sure," Jake said with a hearty smile. "Might as well get the show on the road. I'll pour if you'll serve, Matt."

"Let's get crackin'," Matt responded.

"Great, burgers and beers. Well, the club looks amazing, but I'm glad it's still the same old Barn and Grill," Marcy said.

"I'm with you, babe," one of her jean-clad pals said. "Look, they even left some of the sawdust on the floors. Yeah, this place is happening! I guess it was worth waiting half the summer for it to open."

Matt smiled. Last year, when he had started the Friday night Club Nights, Marcy and her friends had come to every single one. This year, the sky was the limit. Jake, Pat, and Matt now had a real nightclub. They'd left the charm of the old Barn and Grill—the old stable walls, scratched wood floors, and exposed-beam ceilings. But as soon as the houselights dimmed and the colored stage lamps burned bright, the old barn turned into the hottest nightclub around.

Matt could tell that this year they were going to turn a profit. A big profit, he hoped. As promoter, producer, and full partner with Jake and Pat on Club Night, Matt knew that every additional customer meant extra dollars in his own pocket. And, with a little bit of luck, Friday Club Night at the Barn and Grill would soon be joined by Saturday Club Night at the Barn and Grill, too. And Wednesday and Thursday. Matt felt confident that they really had a place that would put them on the map.

But until then, Matt's role as a rock-and-roll promoter would be limited to once a week. The rest of the time he'd earn his living waiting tables and washing dishes, taking orders from college kids and locals, mopping up spilled sodas, and scraping together enough money each week to pay the bills.

But none of that bothered him. At least, not the way it had in the past. Matt felt fortunate in too many ways. For one, he was alive and healthy. Club Night was promising to be a huge success. Then there was his business class at the college. But looming over everything else was that in just a few months he was going to be a father. Matt, a father! A year ago he'd come out here, lonely, missing Julie, just wanting to be with her. So much had happened in the past year, Matt was still pinching himself every so often to make sure it wasn't all a dream.

He grabbed the pitcher from Jake and served it to Marcy's table. "Here you go," he said. "Enjoy."

Marcy filled her glass and raised it toward Matt. "I'm drinking my first one for you and Julie. Here's to you guys." She smiled.

Matt grinned. "Thanks a lot, Marcy."

"Hey, I saw her in town yesterday. Julie's really getting—"

"Big," Matt said, finishing the sentence for her. "It's okay, you can say it—just not to her, or she'll pop you one."

"Yeah, but she looks great. Beaming, just like in the movies," Marcy said. "You guys must be psyched."

"Definitely." A few more customers came in. Matt recognized a few of them from Julie's dorm from freshman year. That blond guy from the swim team whose name he couldn't remember, and a couple of friends of his. So, the students were starting to return after the summer. "Well, here they come, Marcy. The madmen and madwomen of Madison College," Matt said. "You guys ready for another year of them?"

Marcy rolled her eyes. "No. But we'll deal, like always."

"Hey, guess who's giving in to the college side this semester," Matt said.

"Not me, that's for sure," Marcy said.

"Me, that's who." Matt noticed the surprise in her eyes. "Part time, so there's still hope," he added with a laugh.

"Well, don't think we're going to let you live this one down, honey," Marcy said. "I thought you said you were a rotten student."

"Was. I'm going to give it another try. Maybe I'll find out that I'm not so hopeless after all."

The front door opened and a guy wearing a leather vest, a white T-shirt, and torn jeans walked in. He was carrying a shiny black motorcycle helmet under his arm.

Marcy let out a soft whistle. "Check it out."

"Freshman?" one of her friends asked.

"Nah, way too cool," Marcy whispered.

Matt shrugged. "Never seen him before. But he sure looks more like town than gown, huh?"

"He looks cute, that's all I know," Marcy said.

The boy ambled toward Matt and the others. "Hi," he said. "Who owns that great-looking Harley parked outside?"

"It's mine," Matt said.

"Nice bike, man."

"Thanks," Matt said. "Too bad it won't be mine for long."

"You selling it?" the boy asked. "How come?"

Matt shrugged. "I have to."

"His old lady's having a baby," Marcy teased. "Poor guy has to trade his bike in for a station wagon."

Matt rolled his eyes. "It's not that bad, Marcy. Well, maybe it is, now that I think of it. Okay, I'll admit it. I've got to give up the bike and get a car. For the family."

"You? Married?" the boy asked. He sounded surprised.

"It's true," Matt said. Then he smiled. "Happily, I might add."

"Too bad about getting rid of your wheels, though."

"Believe me, I know it all too well. My wife, Julie—she's been on my case for weeks to sell it. 'All three of us can't ride around on your bike! What about the car seat for the baby?' Yeah, I've got to be sensible—part of growing up, I guess. Maybe it sounds dumb, but I think giving up my bike is the hardest part."

"I can understand that," the boy said. He patted his helmet. "If I didn't have mine, I'd be lost. Really." He extended his hand toward Matt. "My name's Bailey. I just got out here today."

"Where you from?" Marcy asked.

"Uh—actually, not far from here. But I just

23

rode in from California. I've been cruising around for the past year on my bike. I've been all over the place. Figured I'd take some time to check things out before college."

"Oh, so you're starting at Madison?" Matt asked.

"Yeah. Hey, I don't think it's going to be as bad as I thought, you know? Nice-looking students and all," he said, shooting a flirtatious smile at Marcy.

"Not everyone's a student around here," Marcy said, smiling right back at him.

"How did you find out about the Barn and Grill so fast?" Matt asked.

"I just asked where the excitement was. Everyone pointed me in this direction. Actually, I was hoping you might be hiring. Any chance of a job? Waiting tables? Dishes?"

Bailey reminded Matt a little of himself about a year ago when he'd first gotten out here, filled with energy and willing to take whatever came his way to get started. "Did I just hear you say you'd do dishes?"

"It's not my first choice, you know? But sure, if you're paying, I'm doing dishes," Bailey said. "This *is* the happening spot, isn't it?"

"Well, he's not bashful, that's for sure," Marcy said. "Hey, Matt, I bet he could handle Carl and his gang when they got out of line. You need him. I'd hire him if I were you."

"Oh, you would, would you?" Matt grinned. "Actually, we *were* talking about hiring someone. Especially for Club Night."

"I'm the man," Bailey said.

"Well, you're going to have to talk to the owners."

"Burgers ready!" Pat called through the kitchen window.

"That's one of them now. Listen, Bailey. Hang out a bit. I'll introduce you to Jake and Pat as soon as I have a minute, okay?"

"Yeah, sure. Thanks, man," he said.

"We'll keep him occupied, Matt. Sit yourself down with us while you wait," Marcy said. She patted the empty chair next to her. "My pals and I will give you your interview."

Matt laughed. The Barn and Grill was back in business.

Marion Green sang along to the new tape in her Walkman as she sat in the barn, doing the evening milking. "Don't feel, don't feel your love no more, baby." Perched on the milking stool, she squeezed Priscilla's warm udder in time to the beat. The sound of the milk streaming into the metal bucket was lost to her as she adjusted the volume of her headphones.

"Don't feel, don't feel . . ." This new band

was great, Marion thought. Totally great bass guitar on the chorus. That was a bass guitar, wasn't it?

Suddenly she felt her headphones being pulled away. "Yo, Marion!" her brother, Frank, screamed right in her ear. "Didn't you hear me calling you? Boy, just 'cause you've been working at that record store all summer, you're like Miss Rock and Roll all of a sudden."

Marion felt a private tingle of satisfaction. Miss Rock and Roll. She liked it. She wondered how it would go over with everybody at school. Would they notice, or would people like Dahlia still treat her like little Marion from down on the farm? Her brother was still standing over her, hand on his hip. "Frankie, something tells me you didn't come all the way to the barn to talk about music," she said. The sound continued to flow out of the headphones around her neck.

Her brother shot her a disgusted look. "Gee, how'd you guess? No. It's your boyfriend. He's on the phone—again."

Marion clicked off her Walkman. "Fred?"

"Of course Fred. Or are they lining up or something now that you've gotten so cool?"

Marion ignored her brother. She felt a pinch of guilt about Fred. He'd called three times in a row, from halfway across Ohio, without her calling him back. No, there wasn't anyone else, but Marion had to admit that it wasn't perfect between them. At least not for her. She liked Fred. Of course she did. He was sweet and smart and absolutely crazy about her. Maybe she even loved him. But *in* love? After dating Fred since early in their freshman year, it sometimes felt as if he were more of a good friend, or cousin or something.

"Tell Fred I'll be right there, okay?" she asked her brother. She finished milking Priscilla, then pushed back the milking stool and stood up. "I'll be right back," she told the other cows.

Outside, the night sky was studded with stars. She spotted Polaris, the North Star, Cygnus, the Swan, and Ursa Major—the Great Bear, or Big Dipper. It was one of the first cool nights after the summer heat. The fields of Marion's family's farm stretched out flat and far, dissolving into the darkness. Marion inhaled the night air, then let out a sigh as she thought about what she'd say to Fred. She'd been feeling pretty unexcited about their relationship since before the end of the school year, but somehow, she couldn't quite get herself to tell him.

"You don't love me anymore," he'd say, a wounded look in his brown eyes.

Marion would feel a pull of unhappiness. She'd dreamed about having a boyfriend for so long. And Fred was the sweetest guy on campus. What was wrong with her? "Of course I love you," she'd say, pushing a lock of red hair off his freckled face.

Now she jogged toward her family's big, tidy white farmhouse. She'd really hoped that maybe she just needed a little time off from Fred, some time on her own over summer vacation. That's what she'd told herself—that if she held on until the summer, things would work themselves out. Well, here it was the end of August, and she still didn't know what to do.

Fred had come out to the farm twice, on weekends off from his father's lab, where he was working, and they'd had a perfectly nice time. Maybe better than nice. Picnics down at the stream in the woods behind town, sweet kisses. Mom and Dad thought Fred was the greatest. "Lovely young man, Marion." "Nice young man."

Marion thought so, too. Still, she felt restless. She couldn't hide it from herself any longer. She let the rear screen door close behind her with a bang and grabbed the receiver of the kitchen extension. "Hi, Fred," she said as brightly as she could.

"Hi, beautiful. Did you see the stars tonight? Ursa Major's awesome."

Marion smiled despite herself. Maybe she was too hard on Fred. He did have a way of knowing what she was thinking. "Yeah, I was just looking at the Bear on the way in from the barn."

"Hey, did you hear they think they've discovered a new star out in the Sigma cluster?" Fred asked excitedly.

Marion had to laugh. Fred sounded like some of the kids at Wild Child, the record store, talking about the latest release from their favorite band.

"A new star—maybe a whole new solar system, a new world!"

Marion found herself nodding in agreement. When you thought of it that way, it was truly amazing. Yes, even more exciting than the latest song from The Sound Solution or Drink Me. "Cool," she said. "Have they given it a name yet? Or is it A-3ZX 134, or something really original like that?"

Fred laughed. "I don't know. Maybe we should send in a suggestion. The Marion system, for instance."

Marion blushed. Trust Fred to want to name a solar system after her. He really was the sweetest.

"Gee, it's so great to talk to you," Fred was saying.

"Same," Marion answered. It really *was* good to talk to him, she found herself thinking. So maybe it wasn't the end of the world if his kisses didn't excite her as much as they once did.

"Were you out doing the evening milking?" Fred asked.

"Uh-huh."

"How's Wild Child? How are Anne and Jerry?"

"They're fine. Work's good." Marion thought about how her friends from Wild Child had teased her about her cute science whiz after she'd brought Fred around to the store. She had a feeling they were really thinking "science nerd." Somehow she hadn't gotten around to letting them in on the fact that she was one, too: that when she looked at Cygnus, she knew all about the chemical composition of the stars and how long it took for their light to travel to the earth, and why some of them shone more brightly than others. It interested her, but she didn't think it would interest her friends at the music store much.

"So," Marion said to Fred. "How's Cincinnati?"

"Lonely," Fred answered immediately. "Gosh, I just can't wait to get out to school and be with you again. Only two more days."

Two days. Suddenly, it seemed so soon. Suddenly, her perfectly nice conversation with Fred was making her stomach feel funny. Marion felt a tug of guilt. She could sense Fred's silence on the other end. He was waiting for her to respond. "I can't wait, either," she echoed. She hoped she didn't sound as confused as she felt.

Three

❧

"Wow, this makes it seem pretty official, doesn't it?" Julie marveled. She and Matt had squeezed all their living-room furniture into one side of the room. The sofa and coffee table and the leopard-print armchair Dahlia had given them as a housewarming present were jigsaw-puzzled together near the door to their little apartment over Secondhand Rose on Main Street. The inside half of the room was now furnished with the wooden crib they'd chosen at Baby World (containing a comforter sporting bright, geometric designs), a changing table that matched the crib, and a chest of drawers for all the baby's tiny clothes.

Matt came up behind Julie and circled his arms around her waist, touching her protruding stomach. "Your first room. How do you like it, Sport?" he asked, bending his head down toward the swell of Julie's belly.

"Sport, huh?" Julie giggled. "Which sport? My little basketball?" She glanced down at her round stomach. "Looks like one. One thing's for sure—it's a lot bigger than a baseball."

"Little Baby Baseball," Matt crooned. "Baseball . . . If my friend Danny's up there somewhere listening, I'll bet he would approve."

Julie heard the bittersweet note that crept into Matt's voice, and she felt a current of sadness. Danny had been Matt's roommate at the hospital while he was undergoing chemotherapy. Ten-year-old Danny had been tough and upbeat right up until the day he'd died.

She shivered. It could just as easily have been Matt instead of Danny. They'd both been sick. One of them had lived, the other died. She covered Matt's hands with her own, as if to reassure herself that he was right here. He *was* healthy. His cancer *was* in remission. The doctors doubted that it would come back.

She pushed aside the seed of worry. Matt was fine. More than fine. He'd just gone out and run seven miles this morning. He was in peak condition. And Danny—well, she and Matt would keep him alive, at least in their memories.

"Hey, Matt?" Julie mused. "What *about*

Danny? I mean, what about naming the baby after him? Danielle, if it's a girl." Danny. Danielle. Danielle—Julie liked the sound of it.

Matt was quiet for a while. "Danny. You know, that might be really nice. Danielle sounds pretty, too. I like that name. I mean, if you're right and she is a girl." He gave a soft laugh.

"Danielle," Julie repeated. "Danielle Miller-Collins." She tried to picture little Danielle lying in her crib, the sun streaming in on her from the windows overlooking the Town Green. Would she have Matt's square-jawed face or her own round one? Gray eyes, brown eyes? Would she have a head of thick, dark hair when she was born, the way Julie had? "Danielle." *My daughter, Danielle,* Julie thought, a tremor of nerves and excitement going through her.

"Just one thing, Jules," Matt said softly, stroking Julie's arm gently. "You've thought about what we talked about the other day— about naming the baby after your sister?"

Julie felt her excitement melt into a wave of sorrow. She turned to face Matt and nodded. "I've thought about it. But Matt, no one else could ever be Mary Beth to me. I couldn't call our baby by her name." She shook her head. "I mean, Danny—well, he wasn't someone either of us grew up with. He wasn't family. I don't know. I just can't see our baby with my sister's name."

Julie felt the tears stinging her throat and rising to her eyes. Mary Beth would never get to see the baby who would have been her niece. Julie would never share the most wonderful thing in her life with her older sister. She blinked away the tears, but Mary Beth's memory was strong in her mind and heart. Would Mary Beth have had children of her own one day? Cousins Danielle could have played with?

Julie gave her head a hard shake and tried to force the questions out of her mind. The questions and the haunting image of Mary Beth's car, charred and crumpled against a thick tree.

"Hey, I didn't mean to get you upset," Matt whispered.

Julie shrugged. "It's okay. I've been thinking about my sister a lot lately. I can't stand that she's not going to be able to share this time with me. . . ." Julie blew out a long, noisy breath. "I'm fine. Really." She wandered over to the sofa, tucked away in its new spot, and sat down. "At least as far as family stuff, things are better with my parents—and they're not so much at war with your dad anymore."

Julie had been sure that her parents would never, ever forgive Matt's father for the fact that

Mary Beth had been drinking at his club with a fake ID right before the accident. Reverend Miller had seemed to hold Mr. Collins directly responsible for his daughter's death—and he hadn't wanted Julie to have anything to do with Matt. It didn't seem to matter to him that Matt was the one who'd really helped Julie pick up the pieces, who'd made her laugh again, who'd whisked her off on spur-of-the-moment adventures—a starlit hike, a picnic, or just a funny movie—and made her feel alive again.

Julie's parents had been furious when she and Matt had become a couple. When he and Julie had eloped, it was the final straw for her parents. They had cut her off immediately— emotionally and financially. They'd told her that she and Matt were on their own, that her college tuition—and all her other expenses—were her and Matt's responsibility now. Even worse, they'd just about treated her as if she wasn't their daughter anymore. As if they'd lost their second daughter, too.

But when Matt had gotten sick, they'd started to see how much of a family he and Julie really were to each other. They'd watched Julie take care of him—and seen how deep their love was. Finally, they'd begun to come around. They'd even been out to visit over the summer, and Julie's thirteen-year-old brother,

Tommy, had reported that they'd called Jerry Collins when they'd gotten back, to tell him how well Matt and Julie were doing.

Julie looked over at the mobile hanging over the crib, which her parents had sent. Plump, bright fish swam through the air, shifting places in the breeze from the open window. Julie's mother had enclosed a note saying that the colors and movement were good stimulation for the baby. Eventually he'd start to reach for it. He or she—little Danny or Danielle.

Matt came over and sat down next to Julie. "Feels weird to have the sofa stuck way over by the door, doesn't it?"

"Yeah, like we're one step away from entertaining guests out on the staircase landing." She gave a little laugh.

"Listen, Jules, I promise you we'll move into a bigger apartment as soon as we have some money saved. With a real room for Danny—or Danielle."

Julie gazed out the window. Out on the grassy Town Green, students just returning from summer vacation crisscrossed the brick paths between campus and town. It looked as if a couple was kissing in the gazebo at the center of the green. "I'll miss our view," Julie said. "I love our apartment."

"Mmm." Matt kissed the side of Julie's neck,

soft and sensitive. "Me, too, but we'll need something bigger."

Julie snuggled closer to Matt and took his hand. "Yeah, well . . . speaking of something bigger, what about your bike—and the car?"

Julie could feel Matt let out a silent breath, like a balloon deflating. "Do we have to talk about that now?"

"Matt, I don't want you to have to sell your motorcycle, either," she said. "But the whole family can't ride around on it. I mean, I'm almost getting too big to fit on it with you now."

"Julie, soon," Matt said. "Soon, okay? We still have almost three months. There's time."

"Matt . . ."

"Hey, listen. Who went out and got you black olives and fudge cookies in the middle of the night? Don't I get a little slack for that?"

Fudge cookies. Julie felt her craving starting up again. Fortunately, Matt had gotten an extra bag that was stashed away in the kitchen cupboard. "Okay." She laughed. "A little slack. But promise me you'll take a look at the green VW we saw advertised in the paper."

"Okay," Matt agreed. "If you'll give me a kiss." He touched his lips to her neck again. Then to her cheek.

She turned her mouth to meet his. His kiss was soft at first, growing deeper, more lingering. Julie felt her body tingle. Her pregnancy made her even more sensitive to his touch. She reached up to stroke his face, felt his hands tracing the curve of her spine. She felt an exquisite sense of love and intimacy. She followed the lines of his collarbones with her hands, sliding her fingers down his lean, muscular body. She drank in another kiss, and another, their mouths searching.

"I love you," Matt whispered, his words punctuated by kisses. Julie could feel the warmth of his breath on her lips.

"I love you, too, Matt."

They undressed each other tenderly, slowly. Their bodies pressed closer, closer. Matt covered her with soft kisses. She let out a keen sigh of pleasure. Matt drank it in with his lips. All sense of time seemed to slip away as they made love.

Four

❧

Julie heard her a second before she saw her. Dahlia let out a squeal of excitement as she and Nick made their way across the sawdust-covered floor of the Barn and Grill to the table Julie was sharing with some of the old crowd from last year.

"Ju-lieee!" Dahlia yelled, pulling Nick by the hand.

Julie stood up and took a step toward her. Dahlia was suntanned and happy looking, her long blond hair streaked even lighter by the summer sun. She sprinted over and put her hands right on Julie's stomach. "Oh, my God! I can't believe it! Can I feel it moving around in there? Hey, everyone!" she said. "Isn't it amazing?"

"I think the baby's asleep!" Julie shouted

over the music. "I'll tell you if it starts kicking or anything. Hey, Nick."

"Hi, Julie. You look great." Nick gave her a little kiss on the cheek. His fine-featured face was suntanned, too. "Leon playing lullabies for the baby?" Up in the hayloft, Matt's friend Leon was warming up the crowd with some jazz on his saxophone. The sweet wail rose to the wooden rafters of the restaurant. "Wow, it looks great in here," Nick added, taking in all the changes at the Barn and Grill.

"Check out the dance floor!" Dahlia said. Through the archway to the new room, Julie could see a few couples slow-dancing to Leon's tunes. Matt had scheduled Chocolate Pie, a favorite local rock band, for later in the evening, and the dance floor would fill up with action.

"Check out the dance floor? What about us?" cracked Scott, from Julie and Dahlia's old dorm. "I mean, you haven't seen us all summer, Dahlia. Don't I get my stomach rubbed, too?"

Dahlia laughed and rolled her eyes. "Yeah, the day you're six months pregnant, Scottie." She went over to Scott and hugged him hello. Then she worked her way around the large table, greeting Bob, Paul and Maya, Gwen and Sarah, also from the old dorm, and finally Fred and Marion.

Julie saw Dahlia's eyes open a little wider as

she took in Marion's new look—black Levis, a white T-shirt, and an embroidered baseball cap pulled on backward over her brown hair. Julie smiled to herself. It was a far cry from the farm-girl braids and Peter Pan collars Marion had arrived at school with the year before. Wait until Dahlia heard Marion talking about the latest bands and albums and all the music gossip she'd picked up working at that record store. Dahlia was going to fall off her chair.

But if Marion seemed determined to update her image, Fred was still the same. "Oh, yes, the sixth month," he'd said knowledgeably when he first saw Julie after the summer break. He couldn't bring himself to look at her stomach, though. "The eyes are opening, and it's got finger- and toeprints!" Julie had felt a surge of amazement. Her baby had fingerprints!

Now Julie sat back down as Nick pulled a couple of chairs over from the next table. He and Dahlia squeezed in between her and Paul Chase. "We were wondering if you were going to make it tonight," Paul said.

"We just got in. Drove all the way from St. Louis today," Nick said.

"The Gateway Arch? Portal to the happening West?" said Maya. She was from California.

"Yup. It's totally wild," Dahlia said. "You know, you've seen it in the movies dozens of times, but there it is—real and in person."

"That's the way I felt out here last winter, when I saw snow for the first time," said Gwen, who'd never been north of her home state of Alabama before coming to Madison. Everyone laughed.

"Well, this year you'll be a veteran," said Sarah Pike. She and Gwen and Marion were sharing a triple in Wilson Hall. Before Dahlia and Nick had arrived, Julie had just finished getting the update on Susan Kim, Marion's roommate from last year, who had transferred to the Juilliard School in New York City to study violin.

"Man, this year we're all veterans," Paul said. "No more rookie act." He nodded toward a table of four students who looked vaguely uncomfortable. One of the girls, a moon-faced brunette, kept looking around the Barn and Grill as if to take it all in. "Freshmen. Remember when?"

Dahlia laughed. "Sure. The Wilson freshman orientation picnic. That was really fun."

"Fun?" Julie laughed and shook her head. "Not for me. I was suffering from a case of major heartbreak. I wound up on the phone with Matt."

Dahlia, on the other hand, had had half the guys in the dorm lining up to talk to her, Julie remembered. Scott and Bob were definitely two of them, and Paul, who'd grown up on the Upper East Side of Manhattan with Dahlia— well, he'd been crazy about her since their days in the sandbox, from what Julie had heard. Boy, a lot had happened in a year, Julie mused. Now Paul couldn't take his eyes off Maya, and Dahlia was definitely a happy, one-man woman.

Nick turned to Bob and Scott. "You guys rooming together again?"

"We're living off campus," Bob said. "With really cool people. And no dorm coordinators to get on your case."

"It's a party all night, man," Scott put in. "Everybody should come by and check it out."

Same old Scott and Bob, Julie thought. Probably the same vintage Neil Young albums blasting out of their stereo all night, too.

"Listen, speaking of dorm coordinators," Dahlia said to Paul and Maya, "what are you going to do when yours finds out about the roommate exchange? We haven't met ours yet, but I'm already practicing. 'Oh, Maya's in the shower. Permanently. And him? He's just visiting for a while.'" She put a hand on Nick's shoulder.

Maya laughed. "Yeah, kind of like having another parent to deal with. Only this one's right over in the next hall."

Dahlia rolled her eyes. "Don't even say that."

"Hey, look," Gwen interjected, making a cradling motion with her arms. "Here comes the happy father!"

Julie half turned in her seat to see Matt coming over with a tray full of beverages. "Hi, gang!" Matt put down a complimentary round of sodas on the table as he exchanged greetings with everyone. "Dahlia—wow, suntan city. You look terrific." He gave her a kiss on the cheek. "OJ with club soda, right?"

For Julie, he had made a special shake of fresh fruit and yogurt and crushed ice. "The Mom-shake," he said, putting it down with a flourish.

When Matt's tray was empty, Nick stood up, and he and Matt clapped each other on the back. "Great to see you, man," Matt said.

"Likewise, Dad," Nick added. "You look good. Healthy."

"I feel healthy," Matt said convincingly.

Julie was so glad that Nick and Matt's friendship had been rekindled. The kisses she and Nick had once shared had almost destroyed any chance for that. But when Matt was sick, Nick had steadfastly showed him support and true friendship. And Matt had accepted the peace offering—after a while. Now the problems seemed to be behind them.

Julie looked around the table and felt the glow of friendship. Everyone seemed relaxed and happy after the summer. Well, maybe except for Marion and Fred. Julie caught Marion staring off across the Barn and Grill, while Fred cast her a worried look.

"Hey, Matt," Marion said. "That new guy working here—is his name by any chance Bailey?"

Matt looked surprised. "Know him?"

"Bailey Smith. He's from my town. We knew each other in high school. I mean, I knew him. Everyone knew him. He was sort of the James Dean of little Spotford, Ohio," Marion said with a laugh.

"Cute," Dahlia commented. Julie looked over at the new busboy, clearing away glasses and plates. Taking in his long brown hair, dark complexion and well-built body, his leather vest and faded jeans peeking out from under his Barn and Grill apron, Julie had to agree.

Nick laughed. "Girls! How about we forget Mr. Dean over there and drink to us? To Julie and Matt and the baby?" He held his soda glass up in the air.

"And to the year ahead, for everyone," Matt added.

Julie raised her glass with one hand and put her other hand on her belly, where Danny or Danielle was sleeping peacefully. It was going to be the most joyous year of her life.

"Come here and let's try it out," Nick said, arching his eyebrows in a half-joking, half-suggestive way. He patted the other side of the big bed he and Dahlia had made by pushing together the two single beds in their dorm room.

Dahlia felt a flash of uncharacteristic shyness. It wasn't as if she hadn't been on a bed with a guy before. But it had never been *their* bed, their home—even though it was just one big room on the sunny third floor of West Hall. Somehow it felt new and different, kind of the way she imagined it might be for a bride on her wedding day. She ran a hand through her hair and settled down next to Nick.

"Looks nice in here," she commented. They had turned the motellike decor into something much homier by replacing the industrial green curtains with new, wood-slatted shades they'd bought in town and filling the room with plants and personal touches. A Navajo blanket they'd gotten out West hung on one wall. Dahlia's Big Apple poster, a tribute to New York that she'd "borrowed" from the New York Transit Authority, decorated another. They'd covered the harsh light fixture with a Japanese-style paper shade.

"Looks great," Nick echoed. "So do you." He rolled toward her, touched her cheek lightly, and kissed her.

Dahlia felt any shyness dissolving in his kiss. She responded, breathing in his familiar scent and wrapping her arms around his shoulders. Their kisses grew more lingering and deeper. Dahlia let her hands slide along his arms, his lean torso.

Their bodies pressed close together. Dahlia felt herself thrill to Nick's exploring touch. Her breath came fast and shallow. . . .

The sound of the phone ringing jolted them apart. Dahlia groaned. Nick pushed himself up on one elbow and began to get up from the bed to answer it. Dahlia suddenly felt a stab of alarm.

"Wait!" She was up and going for the phone before Nick got there. This wasn't supposed to be Nick's room. She grabbed the receiver. "Hello?"

Sure enough, her mother's voice came over the line. "Dahlia, dear." Thank goodness she'd answered the call.

"Oh, hello, Mother," Dahlia said sweetly,

trying to be the picture of innocence. She made an effort to calm her rapid breath. From the bed, Nick shook his head and laughed silently.

"Dahlia," her father's voice said from another extension. "We thought it might be nice to hear that you'd gotten to school safely." Dahlia could hear the disapproval in his words. *Why didn't you call us when you got out there?* Since when did Daddy ever check in on her? He was usually so busy with his zillions of business trips. Oh, once in a while he'd call on the car phone if he was stuck in traffic and had nothing to do. But this was definitely weird. Dahlia frowned.

"Well, I got here just fine. The trip was great." *In case you care.*

"That's nice, dear," her mother said. "Your father and I were just talking about taking a trip, too. We thought we might go to Paris for some weekend shopping. Is there anything we can pick up for your new room?"

Dahlia rolled her eyes. What can we pick up for you? What can we buy you? Well, as Nick sometimes pointed out, maybe it was their way of trying to show they cared. "Thanks, Mother, but we're fine. We've got everything we need. Me and Maya, I mean," she added quickly, throwing a guilty glance at Nick.

"Me and Maya," he mimicked as soon as

50

she'd finished her conversation and gotten off the phone. Dahlia flopped back down on the bed and bopped him on the head with a pillow. "You really don't intend to tell them, do you?" Nick asked.

Dahlia shook her head. "No way. We're going to keep it our secret. Our *cozy* secret, okay? Now, where were we before they called?" She put her arms around him and pulled him close.

Nick brushed her lips with his. "Right here, roomie," he whispered, and kissed her again.

Five

❧

Julie composed the lead line of her article as she walked across campus to Fischer, the main classroom building. *To the outside observer, the first day of classes might look like a cross between a huge party and a giant busload of tourists lost in a foreign place,* she wrote in her head. *Friends who haven't seen each other all summer are shouting and waving over their reunions, while at the same time new students crisscross Central Bowl, their faces buried in a campus map or a class schedule as they try to find 364 Fischer, or the art building, or the bio lab in Kittery Hall.*

She'd just come from her early-morning shift at the *Register,* where she'd been assigned an article on the beginning of the new collegiate year. "You're the perfect one for the job," her editor, Jane Moore, had said. "Our ace budding reporter *and* a typical Madison College coed." Then her eyes had strayed to Julie's growing belly. "Well, maybe not that typical."

Julie and Jane had both laughed about that. Jane had two preschool-age children herself and liked to tell Julie that motherhood was the greatest pleasure in her life. But now, as Julie followed the narrow cement walkways that cut across the grassy campus lawns, she began to be aware of the looks she was getting from some of the other students, and she felt a hot wave of self-consciousness. A lanky, auburn-haired girl stared openly at Julie's stomach and whispered something to her friend as they walked by.

Julie could only imagine what she was saying. That Julie was too young to be having a baby. That babies and college didn't mix. That she was careless. Or worse—foolish. Despite the warm, late-summer sun overhead, Julie felt a shiver of doubt. Was it true? She remembered the afternoon that she and Matt had made Danny or Danielle—drowning in each other's kisses and caresses, unable to stop even for a second, desperate to be one. Uncovered and unprotected, they'd made love as if it were the first time and the last time at once. As if it were the only time.

Careless? Yes. Terribly so. But Matt had just been diagnosed with Hodgkin's disease. Cancer. Their passion felt like the only answer, the heat of their bodies the only way to stop the chill of terror.

Julie hiked her gray canvas bag up on one shoulder and rested a hand on her stomach. Now Matt was well again, and she prayed he was going to stay that way. The love they'd shared that day was blossoming into a human life. Was it something to be ashamed of? Definitely not. She and Matt had given careful consideration to what they wanted—and they'd decided that what they wanted was to be parents. Even if it was sooner than they'd once planned on. Deep inside, Julie felt a flutter, like butterflies in her stomach. A ray of joy and wonder split any doubts. The baby was moving. Her son or daughter was moving!

"Hey, Julie!" Halfway up the long, low steps to Fischer, she turned to see a tall boy with a shoulder-length red ponytail running to catch up.

"John! Hi!" John Graham had been in her year-long journalism class the year before. John looked her up and down and broke into an ear-to-ear grin.

"Oh, wow! I mean, I knew it last spring, but . . ."

Julie laughed. "But seeing is believing, huh?

The baby's moving around right now. Want to feel it?"

John's blush matched his hair. "Um, feel it? Feel the baby?" Nervously, he put a hand on Julie's stomach. It rested there for a few moments before Julie felt a solid kick. John's eyes opened wide.

"Oh, wow! Julie, it's real! It's in there!" They both erupted in giggles. "It's too incredible," John said.

"Yeah, it is," Julie said happily. No, this baby hadn't been planned. But it was every bit loved and every bit wanted, from its head to its tiny, newly formed toes.

"You going to ask Professor Copeland to be the godfather?" John suggested with a smirk. During their freshman year, their journalism professor had been the toughest, most hard-boiled teacher either of them had ever had. Everyone in class had been terrified of him. Julie laughed. "You know, he'd probably kill me if he found out I'd spilled his secret, but the guy's actually got a nice side."

John looked skeptical. "Why? Because he recommended you to work at the *Register*? Julie, you were the best reporter in the class. It had nothing to do with nice."

Julie felt her cheeks get pink. "Thanks, John. But no, I was thinking more about the alligator puppet he left for the baby at the *Register* office. When you open its mouth, there's a little stuffed fish inside."

"Yeah, that sounds like Copeland. The strong shall swallow the weak," John cracked.

The conversation moved on to summer vacation and the classes they were taking. As the first bell in Fischer sounded out on the steps, John gave Julie one more pat on the stomach. "Well, I guess I'll be seeing both of you around. Hey, when's the due date?"

"End of November, beginning of December."

"Whoa. That's so soon!"

Julie felt a tremor of nervousness. Soon was right. She and John said good-bye, and Julie pushed open the glass-and-metal door to Fischer. She didn't want to be late for her first playwriting class. But as she sprinted through the crowded halls, she wondered how she was going to keep her mind on Playwriting 1—or French or astronomy or History of the Ancient World.

By next semester, she'd be feeding Danielle at her breast, or singing to Danny, or walking across the Town Green pushing the stroller she and Matt had on order from Baby World. Julie felt the baby kick again. She was going to be a mom! And soon! Would she know how to hold the baby properly? Nurse it, change it? As she arrived at the door to her playwriting class, she felt a tingle of nerves. It was scary—and exhilarating, and absolutely, totally amazing. Three months from now, she was going to have a child! Let people stare if they wanted to. Julie didn't know how she could stand to wait until then.

Marion blinked in the bright sun as she came out of the library, fresh from her first study session of the year. Gorgeous day. She breathed in the faint scent of honeysuckle riding the gentle breeze. Was Fred here yet? She scanned Central Bowl, where they'd said they'd meet before lunch. She didn't see him. She stepped onto the spongy grass and let her book bag fall to the ground, then sat down next to it. The Bowl was littered with groups of kids relaxing after their first morning of classes. Snatches of talk and laughter reached her ears. She turned her face up to the sun and closed her eyes. A little midday sunbathing—it felt awfully nice.

It was good to be back at school again. She felt so much more comfortable this year, so much more as though she belonged. At the Barn and Grill the other night, she'd really felt like one of the gang. It was great to see everyone again—Gwen and Julie—and Julie's belly, Marion thought with a private laugh. And the two science classes she'd gone to this morning, Chemistry 205 and intro physics, were going to be fascinating. Maybe she'd make some brilliant discovery this year. Or at least cook up a potion for making Fred as exciting as he'd been when they'd first gotten together.

Marion frowned. *Stop it,* she told herself. *You weren't going to think like that.* Hadn't Fred taken her out for a delicious, candlelit dinner at the Madison Inn the first night they were both back on campus? Wasn't it nice to be able to talk about plant growth and cell structure with someone who didn't think that was the name of some new CD release? Wasn't it nice to have a pair of warm lips to kiss again?

She was just going to have to work a little harder at putting the romance back in their relationship. That's what she'd decided. Maybe they could make some sandwiches in the cafeteria and ride their bikes out to the quarry for a picnic lunch. Except that Fred's hay fever had been acting up. Marion sighed, feeling the orange heat of the sun behind her closed eyelids.

"Hey," said a low voice above her head.

Her eyes flew open. And her heart seemed to jump. She was squinting up at Bailey Smith. Bailey, of the sculpted arm muscles and the

59

dangerous smile. "You're from Spotford," he said. He dropped down next to her. Close.

Marion did a mental check of her jeans and sleeveless blue work shirt. Cool enough, or did she look as though she was about to go out and do morning farm chores? She wished she'd brushed her hair before she'd left the library.

"I didn't realize it was you at the Barn and Grill, at first," Bailey said. "You were always more of the 4-H type in high school, weren't you?" He laughed.

Marion felt her cheeks turning pink. "I *was* in the 4-H club," she said a little defensively. She'd made some of her best friends through 4-H and gotten the top award for her prize homegrown vegetables four years in a row at the 4-H fair.

"Well, you sure didn't look too 4-H at Club Night," Bailey commented, leaning toward her. He had deep-brown eyes, with amber rings around them. "You're Marilyn, right?"

"Marion."

"Marion. Whatever. Bailey." He stuck out his hand.

"Yeah, I know." Marion extended her hand to meet his. He took it, and held it for several breathless beats.

"So. What'd you think of the band the other night?" he asked.

Marion's mind seemed to draw a blank. Band? What band? All she could get into her head was a picture of Little Red Riding Hood talking to the wolf. Except that this Little Red Riding Hood was enjoying herself. *Grandmother, what a nice set of biceps you have. . . .*

"Um—the band? Oh. Yeah, you mean Chocolate Pie? Great lead guitarist. Sort of like early Clapton. I'm talking way early. Now, if their singer could sing as good as he looked . . ."

Bailey arched an impressed eyebrow. "My sentiments exactly."

Marion felt a rush of pride. Bailey actually seemed to think she knew something that counted. Well, she'd make sure to save her opinions on plant growth for someone else. And then, suddenly, over Bailey's shoulder, she caught sight of Someone Else himself, crossing the Bowl and heading right toward her and Bailey. Fred! Marion shifted away from Bailey.

Bailey swung his head around to follow Marion's gaze. Together they watched Fred approach. Marion felt a stab of guilt as she saw the confused look on Fred's face. But she brushed her feelings away. Why should she feel bad? She was just talking to Bailey. Talking to someone she knew from home. Fred came to a stop just short of where they sat.

"Hi, Fred," Marion said brightly. She got up and brushed some imaginary dirt off her jeans. "This is Bailey Smith. He's from Spotford. Bailey, this is Fred Fryer."

Bailey got up, too. "Hey, man." He nodded.

"Ah, hello," Fred said uncomfortably. The three of them stood there for a moment, as if someone had hit the pause button. Then Fred shuffled closer to Marion and put his arm around her shoulders.

Bailey's grin just seemed to get broader. He gave a little shrug. "Well, see you both around," he said. Marion watched him stride off across Central Bowl toward Walker Main, which housed the snack bar and the mail room.

"That's the guy you saw at the Barn and Grill," Fred said in a quiet voice.

Marion turned toward him. Fred was looking at her with those puppy-dog eyes again. She knew that look so well. She turned her face up and gave him a kiss. But when they pulled apart, Fred still looked sad. Her chest felt tight. She gave him another kiss, and another.

She thought about the first time she and Fred had kissed, in the outdoor sculpture garden of the Madison Museum. It had been her first real kiss, and the softness of Fred's lips, the warmth of them in the cold air, had sent a current of electric pleasure through her. As she re-created that night in her mind, she tried to kiss Fred the way she had then. Deeper, longer, hugging him tight.

Finally, she saw a tiny smile appear on his lips. Marion felt a trickle of relief. That was better. At least for the moment.

Six

❧

"Okay, so imagine this *isn't* the campus snack bar," Dahlia said, taking a sip of coffee. Nick sat across from her in the orange vinyl booth. At the tables and booths around them, kids traded stories about summer vacation, the first day of classes, new roommates, and where the parties were this weekend.

"It's *not* the snack bar?" Nick dunked an onion ring into his little paper cup of ketchup and popped it into his mouth. "How about her?" he asked, pointing to a girl reading and sipping coffee. "Student?"

"Uh-uh. That's Signorina Gemma. We're in a little café in Rome, and we're sitting outside at a small, round marble table, watching people pass by. There are tons of those little cars in the street, all honking. And lots of fashionable peo-

65

ple out walking. And I'm drinking a *caffè e latte*. And those?" She pointed to the onion rings. "Pastry from the bakery next door." Dahlia inhaled deeply. "Mmm. I can smell the cannoli fresh out of the oven. And then a hint of black tobacco every once in a while from the Roman guy smoking while he reads his newspaper at the table next to us."

Nick laughed. "Sounds mucho buono."

"Molto buono," Dahlia corrected him. "You're going to have to start studying your Italian if we're going to be living there next semester."

"Whoa, wait a minute. Professor Godarotti just told us about the Rome program this morning, and you've got us applied and accepted and hanging out at corner cafés already!"

Dahlia took another sip of weak coffee. The Italians sure knew how to make it better than this. "Well, we *are* applying, aren't we? I mean, Nick—second semester in Rome! Definitely too far away for my parents to be keeping tabs on my living arrangements—or anything else, for that matter."

Professor Godarotti had made the announcement at the beginning of their first Renaissance art class, and Dahlia had barely been able to concentrate on anything after that. *Perspective,* she'd written down in her notebook. *A new way of seeing the world.* But half of her was already

66

packing her favorite shoes and getting on a plane. "Good-bye, Podunk, Ohio, middle of nowhere," she said to Nick. "Hello, Rome, Italy, the world. The Colosseum, the Sistine Chapel, the restaurants . . ."

"All those dark and handsome men," Nick teased.

Dahlia arched her eyebrows. "That, too. So aren't you going to come along and keep an eye on me?"

"Well, of course I am. I mean, if I get in." Nick bit into another onion ring.

Dahlia wrinkled her brow. "What do you mean, get in? You're a straight-A student. Most likely to succeed, and all that stuff. If anyone's going to have problems, it's me." A jolt of worry overpowered her fantasy of the Roman café. "Yeah, I'm the one who should be scared about that."

Suddenly Dahlia had another image in her head: Nick at the outdoor café with some beautiful Roman brunette, who was helping him with his Italian, among other things. And Dahlia, in the snack bar. Right here, in the booth, alone.

"Wait a second, Nick. What if you get into the program and I don't? I mean, I got dumped by my roommate last year when Julie got married and moved in with Matt. You're not going to leave me in a room all by myself again, are you?" It would solve the problem of her parents finding out about her living with Nick, but that was about the only good thing. "I don't want you to go without me." She heard her voice rise. She couldn't help it. She finally had Nick. She wasn't about to let him get away.

Nick reached across the table and brushed her cheek. His touch made her melt instantly. "Dahlia, your parents are big patrons of the arts. You got a private viewing of the Sistine Chapel in the middle of the restoration. Your dad's in big with that guy at the Rome Institute of Art and Art History."

Dahlia shrugged. Daddy knew loads of people everywhere.

"So what are you worried about? You're one of *the* Sussmans. Roma, she will open her gates for you, *signorina*," Nick said with an Italian accent.

But Dahlia didn't find any humor in his words. "You mean, you think I'll get into the program because of Daddy's money. Not because I wrote the best paper in the class on the Sistine Chapel last year. Not because I want to study art history and see all the museums . . ." *Okay, and do a little shopping,* Dahlia added silently.

"Hey," Nick said softly. "You've got it all wrong. You're the one who was just saying you didn't think you'd get in. Now you're remembering the great paper you wrote. See, you *do* deserve to go."

"Do I?" There were always these moments when Dahlia was never quite sure that Nick had totally gotten over his first impression of her: the spoiled rich girl.

"Yes, you do," Nick said. "Anyway, we have to get the applications in first. Six whopping essay questions. Let's worry about the rest of it later, okay?"

Dahlia blew out a breath. "Yeah, okay." Then she smiled. "Well, I better have another *caffè e latte* if we're going to get all that work done. *Scusi, signor!*" She put up a hand as if to call a waiter to their little outdoor table. A girl at the next booth, sporting a purple-and-yellow Madison sweatshirt, stared at Dahlia.

Nick stood up and gave a little bow. "Another *caffè, bella*? I'm at your service."

"Matthew Collins?" the teacher called out.

By instinct, Matt raised his hand. "Here," he said.

Back in school. Weird. A notebook on his desk in front of him, pen at the ready, Matt was experiencing a major déjà vu.

His eyes scanned the classroom. Fluorescent lights, linoleum floor, chalkboard, American

69

flag—in a way it really wasn't so different from high school. There was a nerdy-looking guy on the other side of the room trying to flirt with the pretty girl sitting next to him, and she was totally ignoring him. The students who'd grabbed the front-row seats looked a little more eager than the rest. And, as always, Matt had taken a seat in the back. Old habits died hard.

As on all first days of school, the professor scribbled his name and the class title on the chalkboard. *Professor Clark. Business and Finance 101.* But Matt got a quick dose of how college differed from high school when the teacher then passed out a seemingly endless list of mandatory reading as well as "heavily advised" optional assignments—all of which were due by next week's class. There must have been close to five hundred pages of reading to do in a week. Was he really expected to do all of it? Impossible.

Matt had six straight days of work ahead of him at the Barn and Grill. Tomorrow he had plans to meet with three band managers. On Wednesday afternoon he had his monthly checkup with Dr. Zinn. He had to sell his motorcycle and buy a car. When was he supposed to do the reading?

"This class will not be easy," Professor Clark said in a dry, matter-of-fact voice. "But when it's over, you're going to know a heck of a lot about business. Supply, demand, exchange of capital, and the list goes on. We've got a lot to tackle. So let's begin."

Despite the pressure, Matt felt a little rush of excitement. Supply and demand. Like, a town needed a sprawling nightclub, so they enlarged the Barn and Grill and laid a brand-new dance floor. Maybe school was going to be different this time, now that he had a real reason for being here. This time, there was a definite focus.

On the other hand, it was tough to concentrate when other things were on his mind full time. Like Julie and the baby. It was hard enough being away from them even for a few hours. As Professor Clark wrote a list of terms on the board, Matt glanced up at the clock above the classroom door. A whole fifty minutes without getting to touch Julie's stomach and feel for a little kick.

Matt thought back to the morning a week or so ago when he'd gone with Julie for her monthly prenatal checkup and heard the miraculous sound of the baby's heartbeat. Loud, strong pulses, the promising rhythm of a healthy baby—their baby. And this morning when he'd kissed her belly, he'd felt the tiny being moving around inside her. In just a few months they'd be a real family. Sure, Matt was hoping for a boy. And Julie wanted a girl. But it really didn't matter. Either way, it would be theirs—a precious, beautiful baby. Nothing could be better.

The professor was wiping his chalk-dusted hands on his baggy gray corduroy trousers. "All right, people," he began.

Matt uncapped his pen and started copying the professor's scribbles from the board. Julie and the baby weren't going to disappear on him. They'd still be there, belly and all, when class was over.

Seven

❧

Dahlia sipped an orange juice with club soda as she watched Marion make her way across the wood floor of the Barn and Grill. Short suede skirt, fringed vest over a cool blouse, and a chunky pair of Doc Martens on her feet. What had happened to that innocent little girl over the summer? Dahlia remembered her walking around the dorm last year in those fuzzy slippers with the little bunnies on them. Had she finally gotten the picture that bunnies were just not cool?

Marion approached the table. "Hi." She slid into the seat across from Dahlia.

"Hey, Marion. Pretty nice outfit," Dahlia said. She couldn't keep a beat of surprise out of her voice.

Marion blushed. "Really? I tried on about a

zillion tops and I couldn't figure out what went. But if *you* think I look okay . . . Well, the Sussman stamp of approval and all . . ."

As Marion mumbled and looked nervous, Dahlia had a flash of realization. Underneath the new outfit, Marion was still wearing those bunnies—deep down on the inside, where she thought no one could see.

"So, anyway, I wrote down a list of things we have to get done for Julie's shower," Marion went on, pulling out a pad of paper covered with her neat script. At the top, she'd drawn an umbrella with raindrops and written SHOWER in capital letters. Yup. Definitely still wearing those bunnies. But Marion was a good friend to Julie. *What's more,* Dahlia thought, *at least one of us has been planning this party.* She'd just kind of assumed that a few weeks before the baby was due, she and Marion would come up with a list of Julie's friends and figure out the rest as they went along.

But Marion had insisted on being prepared—or maybe overprepared, Dahlia thought. "With Thanksgiving and midterms and everything right before she's due, we'd better start figuring this out now," Marion had said.

Dahlia read upside down: *Guests.* And under that Marion had written, *When? Where? What time? Invitations. Food. Theme?* Theme? Wasn't having a baby enough of a theme? Dahlia wondered. She gave the list a long look. She could see that Marion was going to plan out Julie's baby shower like one of her science experiments.

"You want to order something before we start?" Dahlia asked.

Marion looked around. "Um, uh, yeah. Do you know who's working this afternoon?"

"Matt. He's fiddling around with something up in the hayloft. And that new guy." The guy with the long brown hair pushed through the kitchen doors just as Dahlia mentioned him.

"Bailey," Marion said, her voice suddenly all high and nervous. She put her hand up in the air, but Bailey wasn't looking in their direction. She put it down. Then up again. Finally he turned and noticed them.

Was that was why Marion was so skittish today? Well, the guy definitely was cute. Dahlia flashed him a flirtatious grin.

"What can I do for you lovely ladies?" he asked, his voice low. "Marion, what's shaking? Looking fine."

Oh, brother, Dahlia thought. But Marion seemed to eat up his corny line. Her cheeks were pink.

"Hi, Bailey. Um, I'll have, well, a root beer, I guess."

"Coming right up," he said, in a way that managed to seem as if he'd said something very private. They locked gazes for a moment.

"Ahem. I'll have another orange juice with a club soda," Dahlia said. She saw Marion follow Bailey with her eyes as he headed off to the bar. When she turned back to Dahlia, she let out a sigh. Boy, did she have it bad.

"Well, he *is* hot," Dahlia said. She saw a sudden look of panic flash across Marion's face. "Not that I'm looking," she added.

"Me either," Marion was quick to echo. "You know. Fred. Me and Fred."

"Yeah, sure, whatever you say, Marion."

There was a moment's silence. At this time of day, it wasn't crowded in the Barn and Grill, and no one had plugged any quarters into the jukebox. Finally, Marion made a wistful face. "You and Nick are pretty happy together, huh?"

Dahlia didn't mean to rub it in. But she couldn't help the sappy smile she could feel spreading from cheek to cheek. "Yeah. It's kind of incredible coming home every day to someone you love. It's so—I don't know—warm." She thought about holding Nick the night before just as she fell asleep, and she could feel her cheeks grow flushed.

"Yeah? It must be nice. Hey, what's happening with that Rome thing? Julie was telling me you guys applied for a second-semester abroad program."

Dahlia nodded. "We should know in a week or two. It was a killer application. Six different essays. At least Professor Godarotti wrote us both recommendations. That should help." Dahlia realized her grip had tightened around her glass. She took a breath and released it. "But I sort of don't even want to think about it until we find out. I mean, what if he gets in and I don't?"

"He wouldn't go without you, would he?" Marion asked. "I mean, with you both just having moved in together and all."

Dahlia shrugged. "If he had the chance to be in Rome, over Madison?" She gave a short laugh. "I know I'd be tempted."

Out of the corner of her eye, Dahlia saw Matt carrying a tray of drinks. He stopped at a booth across the room and delivered a pitcher of beers and some glasses to a threesome of girls from town—that one who always wore denim from head to toe and her friends. Then he came over with a frosted mug of root beer for Marion and another fruit juice with club soda for Dahlia. "Hey!" he said, leaning down and giving each of them a kiss on the cheek. "I told Bailey I wanted to deliver this in person."

"Hi, Matt," Marion said, shooting a disappointed glance at Bailey, who was rinsing glasses behind the bar and hanging them up on the wooden rack above his head.

"Hey, Matt! How's it going?" Dahlia asked.

Matt made an exaggerated motion of wiping his brow with his hand. "Well, crazy, actually. Work, this class I'm taking, preparing for the baby, trying to sell my bike, fussing over my very pregnant wife. Oh, man, it seems like every morning when she gets out of bed, she's rounder than the day before. Not fatter. Don't ever say the 'f' word in front of her. Anyway, we're both good. But superbusy."

"Yeah. Well, just wait until the kid comes along," Dahlia said. She had a flash of Matt walking down Main Street with a toddler by the hand. A dark-haired little girl with Julie's big eyes and Matt's smile. Cute. Way cute.

Matt laughed. "Yeah, I bet when Junior comes along, we'll look back on this time like a vacation. So, is this girls' afternoon out or something?"

"Actually, we're planning Julie's shower," Marion said. "What do you think—umbrellas on the invitations or baby bottles?"

"Uh-uh. I'm not getting into this one," Matt said, backing away with his hands up in the air. "Gals only, remember?"

"Wow," Marion said after he'd walked away.

"He and Julie are really going to be parents. Changing diapers, telling bedtime stories . . . saving for college."

"Yeah, I kind of can't get it through my head," Dahlia said. "I mean, kids—it's so far off for me, it's like it's not real." Still, for an instant a picture flashed through her mind of her and Nick pushing a stroller through Central Park, a little blond baby in a stylish red beret smiling up at them.

She noticed that Marion was glancing around the restaurant again. Her gaze followed Bailey as he carried several burger-deluxe plates to a table of Madison jocks. Finally, Marion turned her attention back to the pad with the umbrella doodled on top. "Okay, should we get to work?" she said.

"Sure," Dahlia agreed. If Marion was thinking about one day having a baby of her own, it wasn't a little Fred, Junior, she was dreaming about. Dahlia was fairly certain about that.

"Sure you don't want to come along?" Julie asked as Dahlia tossed her the keys to the little red BMW. "Watch all the women with stomachs like mine waddling through the aisles at Baby World?"

Dahlia, sitting cross-legged on her double-width bed, laughed. "Julie, you make it sound like you're the hugest person in the world.

What—you thought you could have a baby without putting on a little weight?"

Julie ran her hands over her belly. "A little? When I catch sight of myself in a store window or something, it's like—here's the belly, and oh, here comes the rest of her."

Julie was aware of the heaviness of her body even as she stood in the doorway to Dahlia and Nick's room. The nausea of morning sickness had disappeared after the first three or so months of pregnancy, but her breasts, her face, her legs—everything felt swollen. Her feet were so puffy, she couldn't fit into half her shoes anymore. "I keep reminding myself I've got the most special present coming out of all this, a few months down the line." A few months. Her own words set off a burst of nerves and excitement.

Dahlia shook her head. "You know, I see you standing here pregnant, and I've felt the baby kicking, but I still can't really believe that you're going to be a mother soon. I mean, one day you're just regular Julie—okay, bigger than regular Julie—and the next day . . ."

Julie laughed. "My sentiments exactly. I guess it's not going to be totally real until I hold the baby in my arms." Still, she felt a current of joy at the thought of the tiny, warm creature, snuggled to her breast.

"Anyway, thanks for the invite," Dahlia said, "but I told Paul and Maya I'd stop by this afternoon. Where's Papa Matt?"

"Doctor's appointment."

Dahlia instantly looked worried.

"Just his monthly checkup," Julie reassured her. "Everything is absolutely fine." *And it's going to stay that way,* she added silently. She didn't want to give a voice to even one little smidgen of doubt. Not now. Not when she and Matt had a family on the way. "Well, I guess I better get going. My child's stroller is calling to me," she joked.

"Okay. Sorry I can't come—although with the stroller in the passenger seat, there's only room for one person anyway. Oh, reverse sticks a little sometimes. You just have to baby it. And the brakes have been kind of squeaky for a while, but I don't think it's anything."

Julie frowned. "Look, you're sure it's okay to borrow your car?" She'd driven the BMW a few times since school had begun, but always with Dahlia right next to her.

Dahlia got up. "Sure. You know what you're doing on a standard by now, and I don't need it this afternoon. Just leave it in my spot and put the keys under the door if I'm not back." She gave Julie a hug and a pat on the stomach. "Mom," she added.

A few minutes later, Julie was behind the wheel of Dahlia's little red convertible, the top down. As she left the Madison campus behind her and picked up speed, the early-September wind blew her hair out behind her. Second gear. Clutch. Third gear. Release clutch. She was doing just fine. Now, if Matt would only get his bike sold, she'd be all ready to drive their very own car.

Julie popped in the cassette that was sitting in the mouth of the tape player and hit the play button. Jim Morrison's sexy, rich voice blared out of the speakers. *You know that it would be untrue, you know that I would be a liar . . .*

Definitely Nick's influence in music—he always went for classic rock and roll. Dahlia was been more up-to-the-minute. Julie was glad they were so happy together. She thought about all the times last year when Dahlia had come to her totally down in the dumps.

"He hates me," she'd say, consoling herself over an extra large, freshly baked cookie at DeCaf, the campus coffeehouse. "All he sees when he looks at me is Daddy's last name and Daddy's bank account."

And now they were living in domestic bliss. One big bed, and on Dahlia's desk, a framed picture of the two of them in the Painted Desert on their Southwest trip. Julie smiled as she cruised toward the highway. The landscape stretched out flat as far as the eye could see, but the trees were tipped with the first colors of fall, and the sky was huge overhead, a pale blue with lots of fluffy clouds.

"Come on, baby, light my fire," Julie sang along with the music. "Try to set the night on FI-RE!" The speed and the wind and the music made her feel extra alive and free. She pressed down a little harder on the accelerator. The seat belt tight over her body, she knew that she didn't have too many more weeks of this kind of freedom. There would be other pleasures. But not this feeling. Not for a long time again.

Julie pulled onto the four-lane highway that led out to the Madison-Shelton mall. Shift, fourth gear. A farm rolled by—big old barn and silo, cows grazing in the fields. Julie imagined it was what Marion's farm looked like. She pulled into the left lane to pass the slow-moving flatbed truck in front of her, loaded with hay. Then back into the right lane. Up ahead, the highway curved sharply.

Slow down, Julie told herself. *Precious cargo on board.* She put one hand on her stomach as she pressed the brake with her right foot. For a brief second, she heard a shrill squeak. Then the squeak stopped and the brake pedal collapsed to the floor of the car under her foot. The car didn't slow down.

Julie felt her body tighten with fear. But Dahlia had said not to worry about the squeak. She pushed down on the brake again. Nothing. It was as if it wasn't connected to anything. The car was sailing full speed toward the curve in the road. She pumped the brake pedal faster, harder. The turn was right under her. She yanked the steering wheel to the right, clutching on to it and praying that the car would hold the road.

But as she steered around the turn, she came right up on a beat-up blue hatchback, moving too slowly in the right lane. She slammed her hand on the horn, but she was going so much faster than the car in front of her. She jerked the steering wheel back to the left to avoid smashing into the other car. The car lurched with the abrupt movement. The tires squealed. She was going into a skid.

Terror rose in Julie's chest. The car was sliding, slipping. The metal lane divider loomed up right in front of her eyes. *"No!"*

The scream wrenched from her throat met the sickening sound of shattering metal and glass. Julie pressed her hands over the baby. *Just like Mary Beth. Just like my sister. We're going to end up the same way. My baby and me. We're going to die.* It was the last thought she had.

Eight

❧

Marion headed down an aisle between two towering stacks of books toward her usual spot in the library. Last study carrel at the back, past the second-floor smoking lounge. It was nice and quiet there by the oversize books, and there usually wasn't much foot traffic.

But as she passed the lounge, a glassed-in room separated from the rest of the second floor, she felt a beat of recognition. Her feet slowed down—and her heart sped up. Bailey! She knew it right away, even though his face was buried in the book he was reading as he sat on one of the lounge sofas. Marion took one more step, then stopped.

Bailey didn't seem to feel her staring at him. What should she do? Should she rap on the glass and wave and then keep going? Or go inside? Had Little Red Riding Hood felt this way at the door to her grandmother's cottage? *Oh, come on. All you want to do is say hello.* Marion headed toward the door of the lounge.

A thick cloud met her as she stepped through the door. On the other side of the room, a couple sat talking and smoking. She coughed. Bailey looked up. Marion gave a nervous half-smile and immediately looked away. She focused on the red-brown indoor-outdoor carpet as she made her way toward him. She could feel his eyes on her.

"Marion. Hey. I didn't think you smoked."

"I—I don't. I, um, saw you in here, so I thought I'd come say hi." Marion sneaked a glance at Bailey's handsome face. She could see the amusement playing at his lips.

"Well, hi," he said.

She shifted uncomfortably from one blue sneaker to the other as she stood in front of him. "I didn't expect to see you in here."

"In the smoking lounge?"

"In the library." She looked at the book he was holding, trying to read the title upside down. *Karaoke?*

Bailey looked mildly insulted. "What—you thought I had a motorcycle helmet for a brain?"

Marion felt a hot flush of embarrassment. Maybe she should have just sneaked by the lounge. "Um, uh, what are you reading?"

"Kerouac. *On the Road*."

"Oh." Marion thought she had heard of it, but she wasn't sure. All she knew was that her armload of math and science books would probably seem dull as old dishwater to Bailey. She shifted them around in her arms to try to hide the covers.

Bailey put his book down on the back of the sofa, open-faced to mark his place. "Cool book, but I was kind of ready for a study break."

Marion eyed the spot next to him on the sofa. Did that mean she was supposed to sit down? *Grandmother, what lovely, big dark eyes you have.*

Bailey reached up and took her hand, gently pulling her down to sit with him. Marion felt an electric tingle shoot up her fingers and through her body. Suddenly her leg was touching his, her face was only inches away from his face. His eyes held hers. *The better to see you with, my dear.*

"So—ah, how are you liking Madison?" she asked, her voice coming out shaky. A guilty voice in the back of her head whispered Fred's name. She pushed it away. All she was doing was talking to a guy from her hometown, asking him how he liked school.

Bailey shrugged. "Well, it's kind of weird to

be settled down in one place again." He shifted even closer to her.

"Oh, yeah. You were traveling last year, right? Matt told me. He and Julie are good friends of mine." Oops. Wasn't that like confessing that she had been asking questions about him?

Bailey just nodded. "Coast to coast on my bike. Great way to see the country. Had to work nights for six months first at Bradlee's to foot the tab."

Marion nodded. She figured he meant the Bradlee's near Spotford. Weird. She'd lived in the same town with him all her life, and they'd never spoken a word to each other. Now, here they were in Madison, sitting close enough to—

Forget it! Marion told herself. But she couldn't. *Grandmother, what big lips you have . . .*

She gave a little cough and moved slightly away from Bailey. "So, what did you like best on your trip? The Grand Canyon? The Pacific Ocean?"

"Yeah, they were pretty incredible, but actually, the big cities got me the most. New York, Chicago, L.A. Man, you don't see them locking up the town at seven-thirty at night. It's not like Spotford, to say the least." He put a hand on Marion's shoulder. "So, what's your favorite part of the country?"

Marion felt every cell in her body concentrated on her shoulder, the weight of Bailey's hand, his nearness. "Um, my favorite, ah, place?" she managed to stammer. What could she say? She'd never been out of Ohio. The closest she'd gotten to the ocean was the shore of Lake Erie. But she couldn't very well tell Bailey Smith that her favorite place was the fields out behind her family's farm. No way. Not when he thought she'd put 4-H behind her. Her face burned. "Well . . . I suppose I like the country better than the city," she said weakly.

"Yeah, wholesome," Bailey said. "Wholesome and pretty." His voice dropped to a husky whisper. He was looking at her in a funny way. His hand was still on her shoulder. He closed the space between them. Without warning, he leaned forward and kissed her. Soft, moist, his lips lingering.

Marion pulled back, but she could still feel the pressure of Bailey's mouth on hers. She felt a sting of remorse. *Fred!* He was the one she was supposed to save her kisses for. Fred, not Bailey Smith. The problem was that Fred's kisses didn't feel like that one had, not anymore. Bailey's hand remained on her shoulder.

Marion looked up at him. *The better to kiss*

you with, my dear. She knew she should move away, right this second. She knew she should stand up, say good-bye, beat a hasty retreat from the wolf's door. Instead, she felt herself straining toward him. Nearer, nearer, until their mouths met again.

Matt pulled his motorcycle up on the curb in front of his apartment building. He hopped off his bike, set the kickstand in place, and started toward the front door. As he ran up the stairs, he pulled the wrapped gifts he'd just bought out of his knapsack. A pair of hammered silver-and-turquoise earrings for Julie and a stuffed pink elephant for Danny or Danielle.

Okay, so maybe he'd splurged. But things were going so well these days, it was hard not to go a little overboard. Matt had bought the presents right after he'd been to see Dr. Zinn. The doctor had told him that his cancer was now one hundred percent in remission. As of today, Matt was officially and completely cured. The earrings and stuffed animal were the least he could do to celebrate one of the happiest moments of his life.

"Hello?" he called out as he got to the top of the stairs and pushed open the front door. There was no answer from Julie, and the telephone was ringing. Matt stepped inside. "Jules?

Julie?" he called toward the bedroom. If she wasn't in the living room, eating, then she'd probably be in the bedroom, fast asleep. Sleeping and eating were the two things she did most lately. But Matt could see through the open door that she wasn't in the bedroom, either.

He went to the phone and picked it up. "Hello?"

"Miller residence? Is this Mr. Miller?" a tense, male voice said over the phone.

Matt was instantly on edge. "No. I mean yes. Yes, this is the Miller residence. I'm Matt Collins. Uh—Julie's husband. Julie Miller-Collins's husband."

"Oh, I see. Mr. Collins, this is Officer Larry Rosenthall of the state police."

Matt felt a beat of panic. "State police? What's the matter? Is something wrong?" He could almost feel the tension sizzling through the phone wire. There was too long a pause. His heart skipped a frightened beat.

"Mr. Collins, I'm afraid I have some bad news for you."

Matt's grip tightened around the receiver. Julie! *Oh, my God! Something's happened.*

"Mr. Collins? Are you there?"

"Yes. Yes, I'm here, Officer. What's happened? Tell me." Matt's breath was coming too quickly. His voice was tight and frightened.

"Mr. Collins," the police officer said, "I'm sorry to have to inform you that your wife has been in an accident."

Matt felt a flash of fever followed by a chilling shiver. He could follow only bits and pieces of what the police officer was saying. *Possible faulty brakes. Crash. Guardrail. Unconscious.*

"Julie? Unconscious? In the emergency ward? County General? The one right at the edge of town?" It was barely sinking in. "Yes. Yes, I know where it is. Yes. I—I'll be right there." Julie in the hospital. He had to get there, to be with her. "Yes, sir. I know where it is." Matt started to hang up the phone, then immediately pulled it back toward his mouth and shouted into the receiver, "Wait a minute! The baby! Hello? The baby. Is my baby all right?" But the police officer had already hung up.

As he leaned back against the kitchen counter Matt felt the stuffed animal drop out from under his arm and fall to the floor. He stood there for a moment, staring blankly at the little pink elephant. He wanted to shout. He wanted to cry. But his body was frozen with fear, the tears remaining locked inside. His head pounded with fear. He couldn't cry.

Julie. Julie and the baby. He had to get to

them as quickly as possible. He couldn't panic. They needed him. Now. But the thought of Julie in the hospital gripped him with fear. It was an ugly pattern repeating itself. This time it was Julie instead of Matt, but the images were the same—hospital visits, tears, and despair. Or even worse. *Oh, God, no. Don't let it be.* Matt pressed his eyes shut tight, trying to block out the thoughts. He couldn't bear to think it through. Trembling, he headed out the door and down the steps.

Nine

❧

Matt could tell how serious it was from the moment he walked through the front door of the emergency room. It was as if they were waiting for him. As soon as he gave Julie's name to the nurse behind the front desk, another nurse was hurrying him away from the waiting room and leading him down a tile-floored hallway.

"Please. Right this way, sir. Come with me." Her voice, heightened with tension, made Matt even more nervous than he already was. Something was really wrong. She showed him into a small office with a desk, two chairs, and shelves lined with thick-spined medical books. "The doctor will be right with you," she said before leaving.

"Julie," Matt said desperately. "Can't I see her? Where is—"

"Please, sir," the nurse said. "The doctor will be right with you."

Before Matt could even respond, a young woman dressed in hospital green stood before him. She had a clipboard with her and a surgical mask draped around her neck. Deep frown, dark, penetrating eyes, her face was gravely serious.

Everything was happening so fast. Matt expected her to rush him somewhere else: down the hall, up the stairs, farther along the nightmarish path. Instead, she motioned to a chair and asked him to sit down.

Matt sat down at the edge of the chair. He couldn't wait any longer. "What's going on?" he asked. "Nobody has told me what's really happened."

"That's my job, Mr.—"

"Collins. Matt Collins."

"Mr. Collins. I'm Dr. Daniels. I know how hard this must be for you."

"Can't I see my wife?" Matt heard the desperation in his own voice and saw the gravity of the situation on the doctor's face. "Tell me. Please!" he said, unable to hide his frustration. "I have to know what's happening."

"Mr. Collins, I'm afraid the situation is not good," Dr. Daniels said. "From what I've been told, your wife lost control of the car she was driving. The car hit the guardrail on the highway and flipped over." She spoke calmly but seriously. "She's unconscious. Her body is in a state of shock right now. It's very possible that there's internal bleeding, and possibly rib and spinal damage."

Matt heard the words, but they were barely registering. Julie, unconscious? Bleeding? Almost seven months pregnant and—

"Oh, my God." All of a sudden, Matt felt his desperation spiraling out of control. "The baby. What about the baby?"

"The baby is alive," the doctor reassured him.

Matt breathed an all-too-brief sigh of relief. He noticed the hesitation on the doctor's face.

"But we're not sure about the baby's condition. Some of the internal bleeding could very well be from the fetus. The placenta may have been damaged as well. We're not sure." She paused. "Mr. Collins, it's very difficult to determine both your wife's and baby's status without X rays and other tests. These could be harmful to the baby."

Matt felt a wave of helplessness. "What, then? What *can* you do?"

"Well, that's where we need your help. I'm afraid you are going to have to make a very important decision," the doctor said. She placed the clipboard on the table in front of Matt. "This is a release form. If you sign it, it would grant us permission to deliver the baby right away."

Matt felt a sudden weakness overcome his entire body. "Right away? I don't understand. Julie's not even seven months pregnant."

"We're concerned with both your wife's and baby's safety," the doctor said. "We feel that it would be less dangerous if—"

"Dangerous?" Matt interjected. "What do you mean?"

The doctor's forehead creased. "With your wife injured and unconscious, having the baby inside her could be extremely detrimental to the healing process. The baby's needs will take a lot of energy away from your wife. Energy that should be spent healing."

"Are you saying she could die?" Matt asked.

The doctor frowned. "Probably not. Her condition doesn't appear critical, but we don't know for sure yet. Not without running some tests."

"Tests that could hurt the baby."

"Perhaps."

Perhaps. Maybe. It didn't seem as if anything was certain. "But if you were to deliver the baby now, then the baby might not make it. Is that right?" Matt asked.

The doctor hesitated a moment. "At almost

seven months, a baby can often survive outside the womb. We have an excellent neonatal intensive-care unit here, Mr. Collins. The baby would have expert attention. Its chances of survival are very good."

Matt heard the purposely hopeful voice, but it didn't make him less worried. Neonatal intensive care? Chances of survival? "Then there's a chance that our baby would die."

"Yes," the doctor said. "But it's a slim chance. I might add that if the accident has caused any injuries to the baby, we'd be able to help it now, outside of the womb. It could be a crucial step in your ultimately having a healthy child."

Matt froze for a moment. "I—I'm not sure what to do, what's best. On the one hand, if you don't deliver the baby, it could be worse for Julie. If you do, the baby might not make it. On the other hand, it might be just as harmful to the baby *not* to deliver it."

Dr. Daniels nodded. "It's more complicated than that, but that's more or less the situation. We've been waiting to do the necessary tests on your wife until you decide what to do. I'm sorry to make this seem so urgent, but we can't wait much longer before we'll have to at least take some X rays."

Matt buried his head in his hands. This

couldn't really be happening. Yet he knew it was frighteningly true.

A barrage of images flickered through his head in a jumble of disjointed single frames. Julie—fresh, beautiful, happy—bouncing a little baby boy on her lap. A graveyard, with Matt laying flowers by two tombstones. Julie and Matt hugging each other. Matt holding a crying baby. The stuffed elephant falling to the floor.

He looked up at the doctor. "An incubator, right? Isn't that where you'd put the baby if you delivered it now?" He pictured the frightening sight of a helpless, undersize infant hooked up to a machine, struggling to survive.

She nodded. "Yes, that's right. Premature babies need lots of assistance. If we deliver your baby now, it will be born with underdeveloped lungs and will most likely need to breathe with the help of a respirator. Its digestive system will not be fully formed, and it may have to be fed intravenously. And, because it will be very small, its body temperature will be low, and it will need to be placed in an incubator. But it *can* and *should* make it. Remember that, Mr. Collins," the doctor said. "It should make it. Your baby can live a happy, normal life."

Matt was silent. He felt himself teetering toward blanking out completely. He'd heard too much in the past few minutes. Why couldn't this be a bad dream? Like some of the night-mares Julie had been having about something going wrong with the baby. In one dream, the baby came out as a kangaroo. Julie and Matt chased it all over Madison, but it kept hopping away from them. In another, the doctor told her that there wasn't a baby inside her at all. It had just been her imagination. But those *were* nightmares. This was really happening. Julie's and the baby's lives were in his hands. And Matt didn't know what to do.

He wasn't a doctor. He had no expert knowl-edge of the situation, yet he was being asked to make what could be a life-or-death decision. This could be the most important decision in his life.

"You think it's better to deliver the baby?" Matt asked Dr. Daniels.

The doctor nodded gravely. "I do, and so does the rest of the staff. There are advantages to the baby either way. Your wife, however, stands the best chance if we deliver now. But we can't make the decision for you."

There were still so many questions. Were the doctors here good? Who would deliver their child? Who would operate on Julie if she needed emergency care? What if someone made a mistake in the process? What if Julie had woken up already and was fine? Maybe somebody should check before he signed a permission form.

The doctor put a hand on his shoulder. "Mr. Collins, I know this is a most difficult decision for you. Would you like to be alone for a few moments?"

Matt shook his head. He reached for the pen and clipboard. The most important thing in the world to him was Julie. Without her, nothing else would matter half as much. "I've made up my mind."

Matt looked at the doctor. Her name tag read DR. ELIZABETH DANIELS O.B./GYN. Daniels. Just like the name that he and Julie had picked out for the baby. If he needed a sign of reassurance, maybe that was it. Somehow it made him believe there was a little bit of hope.

Matt took a deep breath and blew out a ton of frustration. "Will you deliver our baby?"

She nodded.

He looked back down at the form on the clipboard and saw a big blue X next to a dotted line. With a shaking hand, he signed his name, making a silent prayer while he did. He handed the form to the doctor. "Please take care of Julie and our baby."

Ten

Roma! Roma! Dahlia repeated it over and over in her head as she ran across campus from the mail room, clutching the acceptance envelope. She'd stopped at her mailbox on the way home from Paul and Maya's, and there it was—a nice, fat envelope with all kinds of information about the semester in Italy, and a letter that began with the magical words, *Congratulations. We are pleased to inform you* . . .

Rome, Italy, home of the greatest ancient civilization the world had seen—and a pretty amazing modern one, too: the home of the Sistine Chapel and the Pope, home of the planet's best cup of coffee and outrageous chocolate *gelato* and handsome men in leather jackets.

"Mi chiamo Dahlia," Dahlia practiced out

loud as she fairly flew toward her dorm. *"Sono da Nuova York."* Or was it *"di Nuova York"*? Oh, well. Practically everyone in Rome spoke English. And what they couldn't communicate in words, they'd get across in gestures and hand motions and facial expressions. The Italians were famous for that. Besides, the semester in Rome included eight hours a week of intensive Italian classes. By the time she got back home, she'd be speaking almost like a real Roman. *"Sono di Roma,"* she tried out, stretching out the name of her new city with a long roll of her tongue.

She raced up the walkway to West Hall and pushed open the front door. Nick had to be coming with her. He just had to. *"Siamo di Roma."* We are from Rome. Dahlia rushed by the open door to West Hall's dorm coordinator's room.

"Hello, Dahlia," said a voice from inside.

Dahlia skidded to a stop. "Oh, hi, Doreen." The tall, red-haired, big-boned dorm coordinator was sitting on her bed, staring out into the hall. Didn't she have anything better to do than check up on who was coming and going? Dahlia wondered.

"How are you and *Maya* doing?" Doreen asked. Dahlia could hear the smirk in her voice. Oh, brother. If she had something to say

104

about Dahlia's living arrangements, why didn't she just come right out and say it? Was this her way of trying to be cool? All wink-wink, nudge-nudge about it? Or was she just waiting for the right moment to blow the whistle on Dahlia and Nick?

Normally, Dahlia wouldn't have let it get under her skin. She and Nick weren't bothering anybody. Let Doreen bug the two girls upstairs who blasted their stereo at three o'clock in the morning, or that geeky guy who was always cooking up something foul smelling in the West Hall kitchen. That should be Doreen's job. But today, Dahlia couldn't be bothered by Doreen. Not when she practically held a ticket to one of the most exciting cities in the world.

"Oh, *Maya* and I are just fine," she said, giving a saccharine smile and a little wave before she beat a hasty retreat upstairs to her door.

She fished around in one of the pockets of her big canvas shoulder bag for her room key. Nick's name was half formed on her lips before she got the door unlocked, and saw at a glance that the room was empty. Her high spirits took a dip. Nick was probably still at the library. She should have stopped there on her way back from Paul and Maya's.

And no sign of Julie, either. Strange. She should have been back by now. But the car keys weren't under the door. Dahlia tossed her room key back in her bag and dropped the bag on the bed. A piece of paper by the telephone caught her eye. She saw that Nick had scribbled a message on it. So he'd come home and left again. She went over and picked up the scrap of paper, torn from a notebook.

Your folks called. Pretty hard to explain why I was here and you weren't. I went out for a snack. Later, Nick.

Uh-oh. Mother and Daddy. Dum-dee-dum-dum. Dahlia frowned. She wondered what exactly Nick *had* told her parents. Was she in big trouble? Or had he managed to cover up for her? Nick could be a true diplomat. He'd probably thought of something smart. She read the note again. Nick hadn't given her much information. What's more, it wasn't exactly a love letter. *Later, Nick?* Holding the note, she sank onto the bed. Was Nick angry about something? Had he fought with her parents? She felt an oppressive heaviness in her chest. What if Mother and Daddy knew the truth? What if they'd insulted Nick? Her parents were experts at putting people down. It was just their style when they were angry.

She flopped onto her back. Already she had visions of putting her clothes in boxes, packing her books and the picture of her and Nick she kept on her desk. There would be a tearful good-bye, Nick standing at the door and gazing down the hall as her parents and Doreen carried all her belongings away. There'd be a stony silence as she rode in her parents' chauffeured Mercedes down some foggy, twisting back road. And there, there she was, moving all her belongings into a great, stone, vault-arched cloister—a nunnery right out of some movie.

Dahlia had to laugh out loud. They didn't let Jewish girls into places like that. Besides, the wardrobe would be much too limited to suit Mother's taste. No, the closest she was going to get to a nunnery was Vatican City in Rome.

Rome! She imagined the aroma of espresso and the sound of so many blaring car horns. Her and Nick visiting the ruins of ancient Rome, kissing in front of the Colosseum. Nick would be home soon to tell her that their Italian dream was just a few months away.

Danielle. Two pounds, eleven ounces.

She was as pink as cotton candy, with light-brown, curly hair. Her eyes were squeezed shut as she slept, her lids scrunched into a million tiny folds. She had a squarish jaw—Matt's jaw—and a full-lipped mouth that was definitely Julie's. Through the glass bubble of the incubator, it looked as if she must be incredibly soft.

Matt stood silently before the tiny, helpless infant. He placed a hand on the exterior shell of the incubator. He longed to feel his daughter, to hold her. But they were separated by a thick wall of glass. Could Danielle even know that her father was right there with her?

Matt tried to hold back his tears as he looked in at her. His child was in another world—horrible, frightening, lonely. A series of plastic tubes ran from her vital organs to a bunch of cold, steel machines. Lots of electronics, computer printouts, and nightmarish blips and beeps. This was her only hope. The tubes were Danielle's only connection to life. She was in the hands of modern medicine.

Her lungs were so tiny—the doctors had referred to them as immature. They wouldn't function without the help of a respirator forcing air into them. She couldn't suck or chew and was being fed intravenously. She lay there, motionless and silent, as if she weren't really alive.

The doctors had told Matt not to lose hope. They'd promised him that Danielle had an excellent chance. She was responding well to her new home. The organs and bones would grow properly while she was in the incubator. With a little bit of good fortune, Danielle would be a happy, healthy, normal baby.

Luck. That's what it depended on. Matt had

never been a religious person, but he found himself praying for it. Praying and hoping. Yet he feared that all his hopes and prayers were in vain. Maybe it was all the tubes and machines that made him so doubtful, or perhaps it had something to do with the fact that he hadn't eaten or slept in nearly a full day. Panicked, he'd paced the confines of the waiting room for nearly twelve hours while the baby was being delivered, examined, and cared for. Twelve hours without knowing a thing—whether the baby would survive, or whether Julie would. Finally he'd been told that Julie had given birth to a baby girl. There'd been an instant burst of joy—a sigh of relief and a proud smile, followed by a Kodak-perfect image in his head of a fleshy-pink, smiling baby girl.

That image had faded fast. Julie had been unconscious throughout the delivery by cesarean section, and the baby had been immediately whisked to the incubator, her first home, where the doctors performed an exhaustive battery of tests for possible problems.

Julie, still unconscious, lay in the intensive-care area down the hall from Danielle, looking equally fragile. Matt had stood by her bed and held her limp hand, but Julie was silent, unreachable, her forehead beaded with perspiration. Yet there was actually good news. Most of the internal bleeding had been stanched, and there were no broken bones from the accident. However, she was still in severe shock and exhaustion from both the accident and the delivery. In a world of her own, she had given birth to a baby girl.

Danielle's tiny legs and arms began to wriggle. Her mouth opened wide in a yawn. Was that a smile on her face now? It was! Matt was sure she was smiling at him. It looked so much like Julie's smile, with her eyes crinkled slightly and the dimple at the corner of her mouth.

Matt raised his hand and waved. "Hi there, precious. I love you," he said. She was so much smaller than a normal newborn, missing the healthy chubby layer of baby fat. A rush of tears began to stream down his face. "I love you, Danielle."

The smile on her face seemed to disappear as quickly as it had appeared. Her eyes scrunched up tight and she began to cry, a sudden burst of silent, aching contortions. Her breathing looked strained, too, coming in short, staccato pulses, orchestrated by the respirator. Matt could feel every ounce of pain that Danielle must be experiencing.

He bowed his head in shame. This was all his fault. That was the worst part of all. He was the cause of this living nightmare. He was the one to blame for the accident, the early birth, everything. Julie had asked him a thousand times to trade in his motorcycle for a car, and each time Matt had found another excuse to put it off. If he'd just done it, just given up the bike and bought the car, Julie would have driven it yesterday instead of Dahlia's car. There wouldn't have been any faulty brakes or accident.

When Julie woke up—if she woke up—she'd find out just how stubborn and selfish Matt had been. He took another look at his undersize baby daughter. Julie would never forgive him. Why should she?

Eleven

❦

Hot tears streamed down Dahlia's face, but she was almost too numb to feel them. Julie in the hospital. Julie unconscious. The baby hooked up to a zillion tubes. It was too frightening to make sense. She pictured a tiny, down-headed newborn that looked like a miniature Julie, attached with needles and tape to a science-fiction array of monster machines. And Julie, pale as the white hospital bedding, her dark hair fanned out on the pillow, eyes closed, no sign of life.

It couldn't be true. *Please, please, don't let it be true.* Dahlia shook her head over and over, engulfed by guilt. "Oh, God, I'm sorry," she whispered, her voice throaty with crying. *The brakes have been kind of squeaky for a while, but I don't think it's anything.* Her own words haunted her with a terror far too real for this to be a nightmare. Why? Why had she been so careless? How tough would it have been to have a mechanic check out the problem?

And now her little convertible was crumpled like an accordion, and two lives were at stake. *Why couldn't I have been driving the car when the brakes gave out?* Dahlia thought. *It should have been me.* She wrapped her arms around herself, but it provided no comfort. Her sobs turned into gasps of pain.

If only I had gone with her, maybe things would have been different. She imagined herself driving her car, with Julie seated beside her. She was pressing down with her right foot against the brake. The pedal broke loose—or whatever had happened to Julie. But somehow, Dahlia was managing to hold the road, downshifting from fifth to fourth to third, the car lurching and slowing each time she changed gears. Third to second, second to first. Dahlia went through the motions in her head. And then just coasting it out, steering way over to the right so that by the time the little red convertible rolled to a stop, she and Julie were safely at the shoulder of the highway.

Only it hadn't happened that way. Dahlia let out a moan of anguish. Julie. Julie and her tiny, premature baby. What if Dahlia had refused to lend Julie the car at all? Or she'd convinced Julie to wait until another day? There were so many ways it could have turned out differently.

At the sound of the door opening, Dahlia's tears caught in her throat. She looked up from the bed. Nick stepped inside and took a couple of steps toward the middle of the room. He looked at her, and his brow furrowed.

"What? Did your parents call again?"

Her parents? Oh, right. Nick's note. The phone call from them. But tears like these would not be wasted on Mother and Daddy. She shook her head. "No. It's worse than that. Much worse." Her voice was scratchy and raw. "There was an accident."

"An accident?" Nick echoed tensely. "Who? What do you mean?" He stood poised to receive the bad news.

"It's Julie. Julie and her baby. Nick, I lent her my car and . . . and . . ." Her sentence was swallowed up in another flood of tears.

"Oh, my God. What happened?" Nick moved across the room like a sleepwalker. He sat down on the edge of the bed and wrapped his arms around Dahlia. His touch just made her cry harder. "Shh. Shh, Dahlia. Let it out. Go ahead and cry." He stroked her hair, holding her close.

Dahlia let the dam open. She swallowed in

huge gasps of air, her sobs wracking her whole body. She could feel the wetness of Nick's flannel shirt where her face pressed into his chest. She let him rock her back and forth. "Oh, God. Oh, God," she moaned, until finally she had begun to cry herself out, and her sobs quieted and then died down.

"Dahlia," Nick said quietly. "Can you tell me what happened?"

Dahlia swallowed hard against a fresh onslaught of tears and nodded. "Yeah, I think so. Just don't let me go."

Little by little, the story came out. How she'd lent Julie the car. How Julie hadn't gotten back by the time Dahlia arrived home. The phone call from Matt at the hospital, his voice so distraught that Dahlia could barely recognize it as his.

"And now Julie's unconscious, and the baby's in neonatal intensive care," Dahlia finished. "Matt sounded so doubtful and frightened on the phone."

Nick let out a loud, long breath. "Wow. It's so scary."

"And Nick, the worst part is that it's my fault."

Nick's forehead creased. "Your fault?"

"Don't you see?" she asked fiercely. "It's because of me. I knew my brakes were squeak-

116

ing, but I didn't do a thing about it. If I had, Julie would be fine right now."

Nick was quiet for a moment. "Hey, hey. You didn't know. How could you?"

Dahlia pounded her fist against the blue bedspread. "How could I not?"

Nick took Dahlia's face in his hands. "Look at me, Dahlia. Come on. Look at me." She looked into his sandy-lashed green eyes. "It isn't going to help Julie or her baby to blame yourself. You know that, don't you?"

Dahlia shrugged miserably.

Nick stroked her hair and her back. He kneaded the tight, tense muscles in her shoulders and neck. "Hey, is it a girl or a boy?" he asked softly.

Dahlia blinked back a stray tear. "A little girl. Danielle Miller-Collins." It should have been a moment of pure joy: the birth of Julie's daughter, Julie's baby girl. But instead, Danielle was being kept alive by machines and fortune. And her mother was, too.

"Well, do you think we should try to get over to the hospital and see them?" Nick asked. "Sit with Matt. Let him know we're there for him?"

Dahlia shook her head. "He said to wait on that. Her family's on their way out right this second, and it's going to be kind of crazy over there."

"Oh." Nick reached over and took Dahlia's

hand in his. It didn't change anything, but it felt good to have him there. "So, what about your car?"

"Matt said they towed it to the town pound, but that I can forget about fixing it." Dahlia shrugged. "Who cares? I don't ever want to see that thing again anyway. I still can't believe I let Julie drive it, knowing there might be something wrong with it."

Nick squeezed Dahlia's hand harder. "Hey, it wasn't your fault. You've got to give yourself a break." He brought her hand to his lips and kissed her fingers. "I'm sorry I wasn't around for you when Matt called," he said.

Dahlia nodded. "Yeah. Where'd you disappear to, anyway? Did you have a scene with my folks when they called?"

Nick frowned. "Nah. Not exactly. I told them I'd come by to drop off a CD I'd borrowed and that you weren't here, so the dorm coordinator let me into the room. I don't think they really believed me, but they didn't say anything. Just 'Tell Dahlia we called.'"

"Oh."

"Look, I didn't like lying to them, Dahlia." She heard the note of anger that crept into Nick's voice.

"I knew you were mad. I could tell just by your note."

Nick shook his head. "Yeah, well. I think you're going to have to figure out how to tell them the truth sooner or later. If Doreen doesn't beat you to it."

"Her," Dahlia said.

"But it wasn't just your folks," Nick went on. He reached into the back pocket of his jeans, pulled out an envelope, and tossed it on the bed.

Dahlia recognized the return address immediately. *Rome Institute of Art and Art History.* But Nick's envelope was thinner than hers. No packet of information or forms to send back. It looked as if there was nothing inside but a single sheet of folded paper. A rejection letter. A skinny envelope was never good news—anyone who had applied to college knew that.

She inhaled sharply. "You didn't get in."

Nick shook his head. Automatically Dahlia glanced at her canvas bag. Her own fat envelope was lying right on top of it. Nick followed her gaze. "You did." His voice was flat.

She nodded, waiting for his reaction. But Nick was silent, his jaw tight. "Congratulations," he finally said. His voice showed no emotion.

Poor Nick. "I can't believe I got in and you didn't," Dahlia said. She saw a funny expression flicker across Nick's face. She had a flash of realization.

"You can't believe it either," she supplied.

"I didn't say that."

"You didn't have to. I can tell." Dahlia felt anger cut through her grief. "You think if either of us deserves to get in, it's you." Nick didn't respond. "You think you're smarter than I am."

"I *don't* think I'm smarter."

"But you do better in school than I do. You're a better student."

Nick raised an eyebrow and sighed. "Well? Is it true or not?"

"What if it is? Maybe grades aren't the only thing they're looking for. You know, I *did* write six essays, just like you did."

"And I helped you with most of them."

Dahlia's anger spiraled. She flounced away from him.

Nick frowned. "Look, what I just said was totally out of line. I'm sorry, okay?"

"No. No, it's not okay. Suppose you tell me why you think I got into the program and you didn't? Do you think maybe it's because of who my father is? That's it, isn't it? You think I got in because of family connections. And money. You thought I was a spoiled rich girl when you first met me, and you still think it!" Dahlia's voice rose.

Nick moved back toward her and put a hand on her shoulder. Dahlia shrugged it away.

"Listen, of course I think you should have gotten into the program. Of course I think they're lucky to have you. I guess I'm just upset that I didn't get in, too."

"Me, too," Dahlia said, her voice softening. "I wanted us to go to Rome together as much as you did." She'd been accepted and Nick hadn't. Somehow, she'd never guessed it could turn out this way. And then there was the awful little voice in the back of her head wondering if maybe it was true—if perhaps she had gotten into the Rome program because of her father.

"Well?" Nick said.

"Hmm? Well, what?"

"Well, are you going to go without me?" Nick asked.

Dahlia felt a wave of confusion. She hadn't gotten up to that yet. Not with Julie and the accident and everything else. She shrugged. Rome, alone? Well, it wasn't as romantic as Rome with Nick, but still . . .

"I mean, I'd go, if I were you," Nick said. There was a bitterness to his words. "It's the opportunity of a lifetime."

Dahlia felt a sting of rejection. "Does that mean you want me to go?"

Nick scowled. Then his scowl melted into a hurt frown. "Of course I don't. Just the opposite. Look, we're both upset about Julie and the baby, too. Let's try to calm down, okay?"

Dahlia felt a new rush of tears. Calm down? How could she? Her parents were onto her, her semester in Rome with Nick was never to be, and worst, by far the worst, her best friend lay unconscious in the hospital because of her.

"Nick, how can I decide anything right now?" She sniffled, trying to stop the flow of tears. "Please, just hold me. Hold me, Nick."

Matt sat by Julie's bedside in the intensive-care unit, still half unable to believe what was really happening. The dismal fluorescent lighting, the antiseptic smell, and the buzzing of machinery that surrounded him only added to the confusion. Matt tried to focus his thoughts on Julie.

Wake up, Jules. Come on, please wake up, he repeated to himself. He'd been there for hours, waiting, hoping, praying that Julie was okay. He wanted her to see the baby. He wanted to tell her that Danielle had already gained one-and-a-half ounces and had grown nearly a quarter of an inch. That she'd smiled at him earlier. But Julie remained unconscious. The doctors had said all her vital signs looked excellent, so what was taking so long?

"Julie? Can you hear me? Jules?" But there was no response.

It hadn't been too long ago that Matt had lain in a hospital bed unconscious while Julie was the one to wait and pray. Matt remembered the moment he'd woken up. He'd heard Julie's voice calling out to him from some dark, far-away place. Confused, groggy, he'd opened his eyes to her smile.

"Julie? Julie, can you hear me?" he repeated now. "Jules, I love you." But there was still no response. Julie's forehead was damp with sweat. Except for a few small scratches on her face, she looked the same as always. Did she have any idea what was going on? Was she in pain? Matt sat looking at her until he began to feel his eyelids start to close. Sleep. He hadn't slept a second through all of this, and his exhaustion was finally getting the best of him. He willed his eyes to remain open, straining to stay awake. He needed to be here for Julie when she came to. But his lids flickered for a moment, and then shut as he fell into a daydreamy twilight sleep—not fully asleep, not quite awake.

He imagined that things were as they should be. There had never been an accident. He was caressing Julie. Her skin was soft and tender. She smiled as he planted kisses on her neck. "I love you," she told him. She turned her face toward his and brushed her lips against his. How sweet it all felt. In a little wooden crib next to them, Danielle was playing with the stuffed pink elephant, laughing while Matt and Julie hugged each other.

He was brought fully awake by the sound of voices behind him. He opened his eyes and saw Julie's parents standing in the doorway. They were holding each other closely. Matt could see tears on their faces. Tommy was standing behind them, frightened, hiding. It was as if he were afraid even to see what had happened.

Mrs. Miller came over to Matt and hugged him. Matt felt her trembling. She cried as they embraced. The sudden closeness with Julie's mom felt strange. Yet at the same time, it was comforting. He felt hot tears rise to his eyes. Reverend Miller put a hand on Matt's shoulder. He stood stiff, a little at a distance from Matt despite the physical contact. Tommy remained at the door, head bowed.

Once again, Matt felt the unbearable replay of just a few months ago. The hospital room, the despair. The Millers had come out when Matt was near death. And here they were again.

"They say it looks as if she's going to be all right," Matt managed to say, barely believing his own words. They all looked over at Julie.

"Thank the Lord," her father said. But his

face told a different story. If his daughter was all right, why wouldn't she wake up? Smile at them? Give them some sign of life?

They all moved toward her bed. Mrs. Miller folded Tommy under her arm, like a baby bird under its mother's protective wing.

Pale, frightened, silent—Matt could tell they were all holding in a world of sadness. He didn't have to be a mind reader to know they were thinking about Mary Beth as they gazed at Julie. "I'm sorry," Matt said softly. He shook his head in despair. "I'm so sorry."

"Sorry? Son, it's not your fault," Julie's father said grimly.

Matt felt a beat of panic. He took a deep breath. "Actually . . . it is." Three sets of shocked eyes were immediately on him.

"Matt, what are you saying?" Julie's mother whispered.

Matt could barely look at them. "The accident. It shouldn't have happened. Wouldn't have, I mean. Except I was so selfish." He had to force his words out.

"I don't understand, Matt," Mrs. Miller said.

Matt told them about Dahlia's car and the faulty brakes. And about how Julie never would have been driving that car if he'd sold his motorcycle and gotten them their own car the way they'd been planning. It *was* his fault, and he'd never be able to forgive himself. "I—I didn't realize. I never thought . . . I mean . . ."

He caught a glimpse of Tommy out of the corner of his eye. His face was blank. Tommy, who'd always thought the world of him. Julie's mom had her face buried in her hands. As Matt's words sunk in, Reverend Miller's jaw tightened.

Matt could see the affection they'd just shown him vanishing before his eyes. They had every right to hate him for what happened.

But then Reverend Miller's expression began to soften. His eyes took on a gleam of compassion. "Don't do this to yourself, Matt," he said. His voice was genuine. "You couldn't have intended for any of this to happen. Don't blame yourself."

Matt lowered his gaze shamefully. Reverend Miller's understanding almost made him feel more guilty. He didn't deserve the sympathy.

"Matt, I think you know that when Julie's sister died, we spent a lot of energy finding fault," Mrs. Miller said. "We blamed your father for the underage drinking at his club. And we blamed ourselves for Mary Beth's irresponsible behavior. We blamed. We were bitter."

"It didn't bring our daughter back," Reverend Miller put in. "Whether it was justified or not. All it did was keep us from making peace with what was."

"And to keep us from seeing the real love between Julie and you," her mother added. "I think we realized that when you were sick, and we opened our eyes to how much you and Julie mean to each other." Her voice cracked with a sob.

"Son, what we're saying is, don't let the important things get swallowed up by blame. Don't make the mistake we did. Julie needs your love and prayers, Matt. Not your guilt."

Matt listened to the Millers' words. Sure, they made sense. But Julie's motionless body, her closed eyes, were more than he could bear. How could he not blame himself? If it weren't for him, she wouldn't be here.

"Juile, sweetie, can you hear me?" her mother was asking. Her voice quivered painfully. "We're here for you. Your father and I, Tommy and Matt. We're here, baby. We love you so much."

Reverend Miller put his arms around his wife. "Shhh. She's sleeping, dear. Let's pray, and give it time."

Matt caught an abrupt movement out of the corner of his eye. He looked up to see Tommy bolting from his mother's protection, running from the room.

Twelve

❧

Born nearly two-and-a-half months too early.
Tiny lungs not fully formed. Immature system
that wasn't ready for the world. It was so unfair,
so totally without reason. Marion pulled at a
blade of grass until the earth gave it up. And
Julie, her body so much in shock from the accident that she couldn't wake from a deadly
sleep.

Marion leaned back against the rough tree
trunk outside her dorm. It was a beautiful,
early-fall day, but she felt as if there were a
storm inside her. Julie and Matt had been
through so much together, and now this.

But behind the gruesome thoughts, there
was the lingering memory of Bailey's kiss. The
warmth of his lips, the smile that played on his
face. *Stop! How can you be thinking about that*

when Julie and her baby are fighting for their lives? Marion chastised herself. But she just couldn't get Bailey's kiss out of her mind. It hadn't lasted long. Marion had jumped up after a few minutes and mumbled something about having to go.

"Well, I'll be close by if you want me," Bailey had said, a smile playing on his handsome face.

Here it was, a day later, and they hadn't seen each other since. Marion wasn't sure whether she was relieved or disappointed. What would she say when she talked to him again? I have a boyfriend? I'm happy with Fred? She'd been avoiding Fred ever since Bailey had kissed her in the library. How happy with him did that make her?

And then the image of the accident flashed through her mind again. How could she even think about boys at a time like this? Her mind whirled with confusion. Her stomach felt as if there were a washing machine inside it. She closed her eyes and made herself take a few deep breaths of the cool air, but it didn't calm her down.

"Marion?"

Her eyes flew open. "Fred." Just what she needed to make her feel even more confused.

"Gwen told me I might find you out here." He shuffled, hands in pockets, as if they barely knew each other. Marion was overcome with guilt. Look at how she was making Fred feel. He didn't need to know the details. He knew something was wrong.

"Okay if I sit down?" Without waiting for an answer, he sat down cross-legged on the grass so that he was facing her. "I heard about Julie."

Marion blinked back a stray tear.

Fred reached out and touched her face.

Marion pulled back abruptly. She hadn't meant to. But she'd done it before she could stop herself. Fred's hand didn't feel right on her cheek. She took in his wounded expression. He didn't deserve this. He hadn't done anything—except be his sweet, attentive self. She sighed.

"Look, Fred, I'm really upset. I think I just need to be alone for a little while. Okay?" *Upset and totally overwhelmed by someone else's kiss.*

"Okay?" The wounded look took on a flicker of anger. "No, it's not okay. You know, Marion, it seems like every time I want to be together, you need your space." Fred spat out the word *space* as if it were an insult. "What's happening to us?"

Marion frowned. "It's not us. It's Julie." *Yeah, and the moon is made of green cheese,* she added to herself.

Fred took a long time to respond. When he did, his voice was low, just barely in control. "Marion, maybe we should stop seeing each other for a while."

Marion felt the automatic "no" forming on her lips. Just as it had several times before. But she pressed her mouth in a tight line before she repeated what she didn't really mean. Even as Fred sat in front of her, she was thinking about Bailey.

"Maybe we should," she finally said. It was about time. She should be brave enough to tell Fred the truth. Well, he felt it, even if she hadn't come right out and said it.

Fred got up and brushed off his brown wide-wale corduroy pants. "I was afraid you'd say that," he said.

He looked so incredibly miserable. "Fred, just for a while, right?" she said.

"Sure. Just for a while." Pain swelled in Fred's voice.

As she watched him walk away across the sun-drenched lawn of North Campus, Marion was surprised at how truly sad she felt. Sad, but also relieved.

Matt stood and stared at Danielle through the plate-glass window of the neonatal intensive-care unit. Her breathing, though helped by the respirator, looked even. She appeared to be sleeping peacefully. Every minute or so her mouth would turn up in what seemed to be a faint smile—Julie's dimpled smile—and her face would seem to light up.

Danielle, two days old, was beautiful. But Matt was afraid to hold on to that feeling. It made him feel only more vulnerable. Something else could go wrong. What if Danielle didn't survive? Or Julie?

But as he studied the baby's tiny face, her crinkled brow, her pink cheeks and wisps of soft brown hair, he couldn't deny himself at least a moment, a brief moment of joy. Even through the thick glass wall he could feel the exhilarating bond between father and daughter.

"Matt! Hurry!" shouted a voice behind him. Reverend Miller stood there, eyes wide open, arms in the air. "She's awake. Julie's awake!"

Matt froze for a moment. He could feel his pulse quickening and his heart beginning to pound with hope.

"Come on," Reverend Miller said. "Come see her."

Matt raced down the hall. The room was a whir of commotion. Mrs. Miller and Tommy stood behind a team of doctors and nurses who surrounded Julie's bed. Matt had to edge his way between two nurses to get to Julie.

"Everything's going to be fine," a doctor was saying to her. "Easy. Nice and slow. Not all at once, okay?"

"Jules." She was awake! Her eyes were open! But the smile he gave her couldn't hide his nervousness.

Julie looked at Matt, dazed, frightened. "Matt," she whispered.

"Can you feel this?" The doctor seemed to be checking for signs of numbness. He poked at her feet and hands. "Feel that?"

Julie nodded.

A nurse was reading her pulse while another injected something through the intravenous hookup.

Julie's face was knotted in confusion. Did she know where she was? Did she see her parents' loving, worried faces? Matt wasn't sure what was registering. Julie looked up at Matt, her eyes begging for an explanation. "Won't somebody tell me?" she said weakly. Tears began to trickle down her face. "What's going on?"

The doctor reached for the tube that ran from her nose and gently took it out. "Better?"

Julie was silent.

"Shh. Everything's going to be fine," the doctor repeated. He stepped back. "Promise. We've given you some pain medicine and a sedative. You may go back to sleep for a while. You still need lots of rest, Ms. Miller-Collins."

"Medicine? Rest? But—"

"Shh. Easy, dear," a nurse said.

"Can I talk to her?" Matt asked.

The doctor nodded. "Gently," he whispered to Matt.

Matt reached for Julie's hand and gave it a squeeze. "Can you feel that?"

She nodded.

"I love you, Jules." He held her hand for a long, silent moment. Her whole body shook with fear. "Do you feel tired?"

Julie shrugged. She looked up at him. Her eyes were filled with fear. "They said I gave birth. I had an accident. Something about the car. I fainted. But I don't understand any of it." She put a hand to her forehead and wiped away some perspiration. "What about our baby? How long have I been here?" Her voice lowered to a barely audible whisper. Then her gaze shifted over Matt's shoulder. "Mom? Dad, Tommy?"

"Honey, we're here. We love you," Julie's mother said. Then she nodded at Matt, as if suggesting the time was right for Julie to know.

"I think we'll leave you two alone," Reverend Miller said softly. "We'll be right outside, sweetie," he added.

It was as difficult for Matt to recount the details of the accident as it must have been for Julie to hear. Her hand went instantly to her stomach when he mentioned the baby.

"I really gave birth?" She pressed her belly, probing, searching. "But it's too soon. It's not time yet." Matt saw the fear registering. Her eyes closed, her mouth stretched into a pained grimace. "She's sick. She's sick, I know it."

"No, Jules, no," Matt said, as hopefully as possible.

Julie looked up. Her eyes searched Matt's, struggling to find the truth.

"She's going to be fine," Matt said.

"She?" Julie whispered.

Matt smiled. "She." He sat down on the bed. "Danielle. Julie, a girl, like you thought." He leaned over and kissed her forehead, knowing his actions couldn't help ease her worry.

"Danielle," Julie said softly.

"She's beautiful, Jules." He squeezed her hand. "She's got your face. Well, mostly. And she smiles all the time. Well, I mean she sleeps a lot, too. Jules, she's gorgeous."

He felt her grip tighten. "Where is she? I want to see her," she said, her voice filled with urgency.

Matt tensed up. He knew Julie could sense his anxiety.

"Where is she, Matt? I have to see her." She tried to lift herself off the bed.

"No, no, dear," a nurse cautioned her. With the help of the doctor they eased her back down.

"Let me go! My baby. I have to see her." She struggled to break their hold, but then her body jerked, and she let out a painful shriek as she fell backward. "Everything hurts so much." She was in tears.

"Ms. Miller-Collins, please try to understand." The doctor was extremely patient. "You've just given birth by cesarean section. And you've been in an accident. Your body is bruised, and the muscles around your ribs are torn."

"What about Danielle?" Julie asked through her tears. "Can't I see her? Won't somebody bring her to me?"

Matt sighed. "She's tiny, Jules. Real tiny." He told her the rest of it. Immature lungs, incubator, intensive care. Two to four months until she'd come home from the hospital. ". . . but they say she's got a great chance, Jules."

"A great chance?" Julie was shaking again. "What does that mean?"

There was so little he could say. Matt held on to Julie's hand. Her tears came fast and hard. As she lay back on her pillow and sobbed,

Matt stroked her cheek. He dreaded the moment when she put the whole story together and realized that it was all Matt's fault. For now, he just tried to hold on to the joy at having her awake and alive. She *was* going to be fine. She really was!

Slowly, Julie's tears began to dry up. Her breathing slowed to an even rhythm.

"Jules?" Matt said softly. "You okay?"

But she had fallen asleep.

Matt knew it was the sedative and that she needed rest. But with Julie asleep again and Danielle in her glass room, he couldn't help feeling a wave of utter loneliness.

Thirteen

❦

Every part of Julie's body ached as she made her way down the hospital corridor, leaning heavily on Matt. Her knees were so banged up, even the shortest walk was difficult. Her rib cage felt as if the muscle had been cleaved away from the bone. At the stitched-up cut in her abdomen from the cesarean section, she felt a searing tug with every step she took. She was dizzy and her head still pounded from the concussion she had. But the pain was dwarfed by the most powerful yearning she had ever felt, and she couldn't help trying to hurry her steps.

"Easy, easy, Jules," Matt said. "She's not going anywhere. At least not right away."

Julie didn't slow down. Her baby was waiting for her at the other end of the corridor. Danielle was right in that glassed-in room.

Danielle. Her daughter. Julie's breath came fast and excited. She could feel herself trembling with anticipation. How strange it was to be walking down the hospital hall to see her own child for the first time. How could she have imagined that she wouldn't even be conscious when she gave birth? How could she have imagined that she wouldn't be able to hold her just-born infant on her breast?

The waiting made her only that much more eager. "Come on, Matt. Come on." She took a few more steps, and she could see the incubators lined up in a row—closed, Plexiglas boxes with so many tubes running from them, like high-tech jellyfish. As she got closer, she could see the tiny infants inside each one.

"Oh, Matt, which one is she?" Her heart was pounding in her ears.

"Here she is." Matt came to a stop in front of the glass wall. His voice softened to a kind of singsong crooning. "Right here, in the middle. The most beautiful baby in the nursery."

Julie felt her breath catch, and she was seized by awe and an intense joy. The teeny baby sleeping peacefully in the Plexiglas incubator was perfect, from her curly, light-brown hair to her tiny button nose, to her pudgy stomach protruding from her diaper, to her padded hands and feet, the nails like miniature seed pearls.

Julie stared, hardly daring to believe this was her baby. "Oh, my darling," she whispered. "My sweet Danielle." Tears of happiness rose to her eyes. She hardly noticed the tubes running out of Danielle's little arms and legs and body. "Matt, she looks like you—something about the shape of her face, her chin."

"Yeah? I thought she looked more like you. Especially her mouth. You'll see it when she wakes up. Hey, did you notice she's the only one with a full head of hair?"

Julie glanced at the other babies near Danielle. Though their bodies were covered with a layer of soft-looking down, typical of premature babies, two of them were bald as eggs on top, one sported a curl or two, one a downy fuzz of hair. They were all so tiny, so fragile. But Julie's gaze was pulled back to her daughter almost immediately. She couldn't bear to take her eyes off her for a second. She put her hand up against the glass in front of Danielle, longing with every fiber of her being to feel her daughter's soft skin, to hold her tiny hands.

Matt put his arm around Julie. "Come on," he said.

Julie felt a tidal wave of resistance. "What do you mean? We just got here."

Matt laughed. "No, no. I mean, let's go inside. I thought you might want to touch her."

"Really, I can?"

Matt nodded. "Well, not with your bare hands—it's a sterile environment in there—but see those holes in the sides of the incubator?"

There was a large, round hole on each side of the Plexiglas box that held Danielle, and another one by her head. Sealed inside each hole was a latex sleeve that ended in a glove.

"That's how they care for her, change her, feed her," Matt explained.

A few moments later, assisted by a nurse, Julie was putting her hands into the gloves and reaching into Danielle's sterile home. "Won't I wake her up?" Julie whispered, her eyes on Danielle's face.

The nurse smiled. "I'll bet she won't mind waking up to see her mother. She can go back to sleep. Just be extra careful not to touch any of the tubes."

Her hands shaking, Julie gingerly placed a hand on Danielle's head. As soon as her fingers made contact, she felt a wild surge of love like nothing she'd ever experienced. *My flesh and blood,* she thought, the expression carrying a meaning she suddenly realized she'd never fully understood before.

She cradled Danielle's head and her cheek. The baby's face scrunched up as her tiny mouth opened wide in a yawn. Then her eyes opened. She was looking right at Julie!

Julie felt as if she might faint from happiness. "My love," she whispered.

She touched Danielle's arm. Even through the latex glove, she could feel how soft she was.

Stay away from the tubes, she reminded herself. Her joy was dampened as she took a closer look at the paper tape, only partially concealing the needles that attached the tubes and monitors to Danielle's body.

"You okay?" Matt whispered.

Julie sighed. "She should be in our arms."

"And it's my fault she's not," Matt said.

Julie felt a tug of surprise. "Your fault?"

"Because I didn't sell my bike. Buy us a car—with working brakes."

Julie felt the meaning of Matt's words creeping over her. If he'd only been less resistant about parting with his motorcycle, she might have been in their own car, not Dahlia's. On the other hand, she still would have been driving too fast, reveling in her own sense of freedom instead of thinking about the special, special person she was carrying inside her. Matt's fault? Her own fault? Julie felt Danielle's tiny body warm under her gloved hands. Maybe it didn't matter, as long as Danielle came home safe and sound.

"Matt, I don't blame you," Julie said.

"You don't?"

She shook her head, moving her hand to Danielle's hand. She put her glove-cloaked index finger in Danielle's fleshy palm, and the infant closed her hand around it. Any bad feelings were swept away by the most acute wonder and joy.

"You know the doctors say she's doing well," Julie said. "As soon as her lungs start getting stronger, we're going to be bringing her home, wrapped in a yellow blanket, just like we planned." She closed her eyes for a moment, strengthening her words with a silent prayer. *Yes, please. Soon.*

When she opened her eyes and looked at her daughter again, she saw Danielle's mouth form what seemed to be a smile. "Oh, Matt, look! She's smiling." Julie could feel her own enormous smile. *Soon we're going to be bringing her home. . . .*

Here she is. Little Red Riding Hood, arm in arm with the wolf, Marion thought. Was she crazy to have accepted Bailey's last-minute invitation to an off-campus party? After not hearing from him for four days, four hours, and some-odd minutes since they'd kissed in the library? *But who's counting?*

As they left North Campus and headed down the narrow sidewalk on Elm Street, Bailey drew Marion closer. "I'm glad you came tonight," he said in a throaty voice.

Marion felt a trill of pleasure. "You are?" She could feel his perfect arm muscles through his leather jacket.

"Yeah, you look great." He stopped walking for a moment and pulled back to look at her in her black leggings, oversize sweater, and suede ankle boots. His eyes moving over her were almost like a tingly touch.

Bailey slung his arm around her shoulders and she snuggled closer to him as they began walking again. There was something about knowing that Bailey wasn't the sensible choice that made it even more exciting to be with him. There was a feeling of mystery and adventure. The briskness of the evening air only highlighted it. The moon, almost full, had a halo of fog around it.

"So, whose party is it we're going to?" Marion asked. "Will I know anyone?"

"Well, the people who are throwing it are seniors," Bailey said. "Sharon something or other and her housemates."

Marion shrugged. "I don't know too many seniors. How do you know her?"

"Barn and Grill. You meet all kinds of people

145

working there. If you've got to work, it's the place."

"Yeah, I kind of felt that way about the record store this summer," Marion said. She felt slightly less nervous as she and Bailey fell into a surprisingly easy conversation.

"Wild Child, right? I used to hang out there sometimes when I was living in Spotford." Bailey made it sound as if he'd been out of their hometown for years. Of course, with all the places he'd seen since he'd left home, it must have felt that way, Marion reasoned.

She tried to imagine herself pulling away from the farm in the old green Ford that her family used as a second car, a road atlas next to her, with everything she'd need for many months on the road packed into the trunk. What would it be like to wake up every morning in a strange motel room, or stretched out on the backseat of the car—all alone in a place she had never been before? The open road would lie ahead every day, in any direction she happened to want to go. The glitter of New Orleans, the vast peace of the Rocky Mountains, the history of old New England. She felt a strange, compelling combination of freedom and fear.

Fantasies of new experiences playing at the edges of her mind, Marion was vaguely aware of the familiar figure coming toward her and

Bailey. Then her realization sharpened. *Oh, my God. It's Fred.* All of a sudden, she was back on Elm Street, Madison, Ohio. She broke away from Bailey's touch.

"Here's Fred," she whispered to him, and a brief moment later, Fred was right in front of them. "Hi, Fred." Her voice came out high and nervous. She'd been caught.

In the play of moonlight, Marion saw Fred's face crinkle miserably. "Hi, Marion." His voice was barely audible. There was a moment of awkward silence. Then he stepped off the sidewalk, edged around her and Bailey, and kept walking in the other direction.

Marion felt a sudden wave of despair and sadness. That was it? Fred had been her boyfriend and best friend for almost a year, and they could barely say a word to each other? A part of her wanted to whirl around and run after him. Put her arms around him and kiss away the unhappiness from his freckled face.

But the other part of her knew that she'd just wind up feeling trapped again. It was time for something new. For an adventure. And Bailey was it.

"You okay?" he asked, surprising her with his concern.

She nodded.

"It's going to be a hot party. Sharon said lots

of good food, dancing . . . And maybe after, we can spend some private time together. Go for a ride on my bike. Whatever . . . If you want to," he added.

Marion slipped her arm around Bailey's waist. He gave her a sure hug. "I think I'll want to," she said.

Fourteen

❧

Julie stepped outside for the first time in over
two weeks. She blinked in the crisp fall sun, her
eyes adjusting to the brightness. It was notice-
ably colder than before she'd gone into the hospital.

Before. Before she'd set out in Dahlia's car,
before the accident. The road divider loomed
up in her mind, just the way it had before the
car had hit it. Somehow, the image got mixed
up with the one she had of Mary Beth's car,
crushed against that huge tree.

Julie shivered and wrapped her arms
around her stomach. It felt so strange. There
was no longer a baby protected inside a swollen
belly. She automatically glanced back at the
modern brick hospital building, and up at the
second floor. Now her baby was in there some-

where—without her. Julie was seized by the urge to run back inside.

"Jules?" Matt said gently. "You doing all right?"

Julie bit her lip to keep from crying.

"It's a beautiful day, isn't it?" Matt pointed out.

Julie nodded. Usually, fall was her favorite season. A hint of whatever lay ahead hung on the wood-smoke-scented air—whatever lay ahead after a lazy summer. She loved the bite in the air, the way the cold stung her nostrils. It made her think of hot chocolate and fresh apples and warm doughnuts, long bike rides and brilliant, falling leaves swirling through the sky. But right now, she would trade all of that in a split second to race right back into the season-less, fluorescent stuffiness of the hospital to see her daughter's face for just a moment.

"Sweetheart, here's the cab I called to take us back home," Matt said. He urged her toward the curb, where a sleek black car was waiting.

Julie took a reluctant step toward the taxi. "How'd you get here?" she asked.

"Walked. It's such a gorgeous day, and I didn't get to take a run this morning. Hey, you coming?"

Julie could tell Matt was trying hard to be upbeat. But she followed his gaze as he, too, stole a look up at the second floor of the hospital. The neonatal ward was over there on the right, wasn't it? Julie felt a tug of misery. "My baby is in there and I'm just waltzing away." It wasn't supposed to be like this. She and Matt were supposed to be bringing Danielle home with them, all wrapped up in the yellow blanket they'd bought just for the occasion.

"Julie, I have news for you. You're not waltzing," Matt said. Julie could hear the deliberate lightness in his tone. "Not in your condition, you're not."

Julie tried to laugh. The little noise in her throat came out more like a pathetic bleat. Without warning, it turned into a sob.

"Hey, hey." Matt put his arms around her and gave her a hug. "Oops, am I squeezing your ribs too hard?"

Blinking away tears, Julie shook her head, even though it did hurt. The doctors had said it could take weeks, months even, to fully heal, but she desperately needed the hug. She buried her face in Matt's chest, breathing in the faintly soapy smell of his sweater.

"She's getting the best care," Matt murmured. "I don't want to leave her, either, but we're going to come see her every single day. Every day until her lungs get strong enough and we bring her home."

"Yeah." Julie sniffled. "But when we're not there . . ."

"Jules, don't you think Nurse Fleming has taken a kind of special liking to Danielle?"

Julie shrugged. Nurses, doctors. What an unfair way to begin life.

Matt kissed Julie's brow. "Look, it's hard for me to leave her, too. Incredibly hard. But we can't spend every minute standing at the neonatal ward staring through a sheet of glass. You know that, Jules. We have jobs, classes . . ."

Julie heard Matt's words, but she couldn't feel them. "Matt, we have a *daughter* . . ."

Matt let go of her. He nodded, the most serious expression on his square-jawed face. "Yes, we do. We have a daughter, and she's alive. Alive and loved, and the doctors say that if all goes well, we'll have her home by Thanksgiving."

Julie felt a surge of hope. "That would be the biggest thing to be thankful for," she said. Danielle lying in her crib at home as Julie basted the turkey. Danielle cooing as Matt rocked her in his arms. Julie turned her face up to feel the crisp sunshine. "Did I tell you that my parents said they might come out again for Thanksgiving and spend it with us?"

"That would be nice," Matt said. "A real family Thanksgiving."

"Maybe I could do a better job with the food this year," Julie commented, a real smile actually forming on her lips. "I think we've both gotten better in the kitchen, huh?" Last year's Thanksgiving dinner had been a total fiasco.

Matt laughed, too. "Yeah. That's what I like to see. A real smile—a real Julie smile." He traced her mouth gently with his fingertip.

Julie felt her smile dissolve into a sigh. "But, Matt, it's so hard. Here we are outside, laughing, and it's a beautiful day—and Danielle's in a little box in there."

Matt frowned. "I know. Believe me, I know. But we've got to think positive. It's the only way, Jules. It won't be too long before we can take her home, just the way we imagined."

"In the yellow blanket?"

"What else?" Matt took Julie's arm and led her to the waiting taxi. "You know, it's really a miracle that both my girls are going to be fine," he said.

Professor Yorowitz was taking the class through the tombs of ancient Egypt, but Julie sat at her desk imagining herself giving Danielle a bath. She'd undress her and put her in the blue plastic baby tub on the counter next to the kitchen sink. Bare hands against Danielle's bare skin—no latex glove between them.

Just flesh and blood and warmth and love. Then, cup by gentle cupful, she'd pour warm water into the tub and sponge it all over her daughter's soft little body. She imagined Danielle giggling with ticklish delight.

The moment seemed closer and closer. When she'd visited Danielle this morning, her daughter had looked even bigger and chubbier than she had yesterday. And Julie was getting a little stronger every day, too. Soon. Soon.

But until then, you've got to come back down to planet Earth, Julie reminded herself, trying to rejoin the rest of the class and her professor's lecture. It was hopeless. Joyous motherhood consumed her thoughts.

"Nobody quite understands how the tombs were built," he was saying. "Even with our modern technology, it would be a feat."

Julie wrote that down in her notebook. While she'd been in the hospital, she'd managed to miss all of Mesopotamia and the first part of ancient Egypt. In addition to hundreds of years of ancient history, she was scrambling to catch up in all her other classes, to do as much as possible before Danielle came home.

Danielle. Danielle. Beautiful brown hair and sparkling eyes, perfect little mouth, her father's chin but her mother's smile. Julie couldn't help thinking about the day she'd dress her in the totally adorable miniature overalls Dahlia had bought for her, or tuck her into her little crib. She couldn't bear the thought of another day apart from her. No, after classes today, she'd convince Matt to take a ride out to the hospital for a late-afternoon visit. She knew Matt wouldn't be able to resist, either.

Professor Yorowitz was unraveling the mysteries of Egypt. She took a deep breath and tried to concentrate on what he was saying. *Soon,* she told herself. Soon she and Matt and Danielle would be a real family.

Fifteen

🙠

Marion and Bailey. That guy Bailey and Marion with her fuzzy bunny slippers. Dahlia couldn't believe it. She had just seen Marion riding around on the back of Bailey's motorcycle with her hands around his waist. Shy, innocent farm girl turned biker chick! Dahlia was bursting with the news as she pushed open the door to her room.

"Nick, you won't believe what—" Dahlia stopped in midsentence as she saw Nick on the telephone. He turned around, receiver in hand, as she stepped into the room.

"Well, here she is now. Maybe she can explain it herself," she heard him say. Without another word, he held out the phone to her as if it were a poisonous snake.

"Who is it?" she mouthed.

Nick just continued to hold the receiver out to her.

Dahlia frowned as she took it. "Hello?"

"And why is it that every time we call you, your friend Nick just happens to be in the room? Even when you're not. Do you have anything to say about that, young lady?"

Brother. Dahlia took the phone and carried it over to the bed. Mother and Daddy had to be onto her; otherwise they never would have bothered to call so often. "And hello to you, too, Daddy," she said, plopping down on the bed.

"Dahlia, I'm quite serious. How is it that Maya never picks up the telephone?"

"Well, Daddy, if you want her to call you when she gets in, I'll tell her. I'm sure the two of you will have a nice little chat."

"Dahlia, I'm warning you . . ."

Dahlia looked over at Nick and rolled her eyes. But Nick, sitting sideways in his desk chair, didn't give her any sign of sympathy. Daddy kept on going.

"Now, I don't want to have to come out there and find out that you're paying more attention to your love life than to your academic life. Is that understood?"

"Daddy," Dahlia said in her sweetest voice, "I'm not sure I do. Nick's over here visiting, and Maya's out. That's not illegal, is it?"

Her father made a noise of impatience. "Visiting, is that it? Dahlia, your mother and I sent you to college for a reason, and that reason was *not* to experiment in alternative life-styles."

"Alternative life-styles? Daddy, I think that was back in your time," Dahlia said. Why didn't the guy get off her case?

"I think you catch my drift," he said, using another one of his hokey sixties expressions. If only he could remember all that stuff about free love. But Dahlia had a feeling that he and her mother had just been in it for the cool clothes. Threads, they used to call them.

"Daddy, if you're suggesting that I'm living with Nick, I'm not," Dahlia said, crossing her fingers. She'd hoped it wouldn't come down to having to tell an out-and-out lie, but what choice did she have?

Nick shot her a disgusted look.

"Well, I hope you're telling me the truth," her father said grimly. "Because if I find out you haven't been straight with me . . ." He didn't finish his sentence. He didn't have to.

Power to the pocketbook, Dahlia thought bitterly. Maybe the best thing that could happen would be for him and Mother to find out the real story. Let them cut her off again. Then she wouldn't owe them a thing. Not one single thing. She'd be free. Of course, she'd have a hard time getting to Rome if she were *that* free.

She clenched her teeth and listened to Daddy move on to business in New York, the preholiday season, and the fabulous new restaurant that had opened right around the corner. Then her mother got on the phone and basically repeated the same thing. "Marvelous fresh river trout," she said. "Simply fabulous. Now, about that boy—Nick . . ."

Dahlia went through it all over again. When she finally hung up, she let out a loud groan. Nick was still watching her from his chair.

"Well, I guess if you want to get to Italy, you might have to find a job as a flight attendant," he said.

Dahlia felt stung. There wasn't a trace of humor in Nick's voice. "Very funny. You want to make sure my parents find out so they'll cut me off again? That's one way to guarantee that I'll stay here with you," she shot back. She was sorry the second the words were out of her mouth. Nick's face crumpled up with hurt.

"Dahlia, no one's forcing you to stick around. I'd just like to know what you're doing, okay?" His green eyes flashed. "I have to live with you every day, and I have no idea if you're going to be around after January."

"*Have* to live with me? Who's forcing

whom?" Dahlia blew out a breath of annoyance. "Anyway, Nick, notice I didn't say anything about Rome to Daddy and Mother yet. Did you ever think it's because maybe I'd prefer to stick around boring little Madison—because there's someone I really care about here?"

She could see Nick's expression soften. She felt her own anger deflating, too. She didn't want to fight with Nick. Far from it. She patted the bed next to her. "Hey, why don't you come over here and visit me?"

Nick shrugged. Dahlia waited for him to relent. She could already imagine the feel of his lips on hers. Kiss and make up. Yum. But instead of getting up and coming over to her, he swiveled around in his chair and opened a fat textbook on his desk.

Dahlia's disappointment mingled with a fresh current of anger. If she was lying to her parents about Nick, it was because she wanted to be with him. And if she couldn't decide about next semester, it was for the same reason. Didn't the guy understand how hard it was to choose Madison over Rome? And that if she was thinking about doing it, it was all because of him? But it felt as if Nick was pushing her away. Pushing her right onto that plane.

She flopped onto her back and stared at the ugly, fiberboard ceiling. Why did Nick have to be so envious and jealous of her? Couldn't he be happy that one of them had this fabulous opportunity? Nick could be the sweetest, most interesting, sexiest guy in the whole world. But he could also be the most stubborn and impossible. Just like on that first, awful road trip back to New York last year. Maybe she should have learned her lesson back then. Dahlia didn't even want to tell Nick about Marion and Bailey anymore.

Julie raced down the hospital corridor, despite the ache of her still-healing injuries, and stopped in front of Danielle's incubator. Her anticipation turned to confusion as she saw that the Plexiglas cubicle was empty. She glanced around the nursery. Had they moved her to another part of the room? There was the baby boy who'd just been born a few days earlier, even tinier than Danielle had been at birth. There was spunky little Charlotte, who'd been born with a serious kidney problem. But no sign of Danielle.

"She's not here," Julie said as Matt came up behind her. She spotted Nurse Fleming coming out of the room behind the nursery, and she rapped on the glass.

Nurse Fleming's expression stopped Julie's heart cold. The nurse seemed to swallow a little gasp. She bit her lip and cast her gaze downward. Julie's hand froze in mid-greeting. A lump of wild terror rising to her throat, she watched Nurse Fleming disappear into the back room and reappear almost immediately with Dr. Daniels. Dr. Daniels's face was grim.

The nurse and the doctor walked briskly toward the door of the nursery. Automatically, numbly, Julie felt herself moving toward them.

"Where's Danielle?" she asked the moment Dr. Daniels and Nurse Fleming had stepped out into the corridor.

"We just tried to call you," Dr. Daniels said.

Julie felt Matt put his arm around her. She felt as if she were back in Dahlia's car, skidding toward disaster, and there wasn't a thing she could do to stop it. She was seized with the urge to clamp her hands over her ears.

"I'm so sorry, Julie, Matt. She didn't make it," the doctor said.

Julie stood motionless. It was as if she were hearing the words from very far away, through a long, long tunnel. Matt's arm tightened around her, and she heard him let out a low moan. That seemed far away, too.

"Her lungs just weren't strong enough," the doctor said.

"We really thought she'd pull through,"

Nurse Fleming added, her voice teary. "She was so close."

"No," Julie said, the sound barely escaping her lips. It wasn't true. Danielle had come so far already.

"We think she developed a sudden acute flu and congestion," Dr. Daniels was saying, "and that her lungs were too fragile to handle it."

No, it wasn't true. It couldn't be. "Where is she?" Julie heard herself saying, almost as if she were two people, one of them standing back and watching from a place no pain could touch.

"God, no," Matt echoed, his voice trembling.

Nurse Fleming stepped forward. "Maybe you two should sit down," she said gently.

Julie looked toward the spot where Danielle was supposed to be lying in her incubator. "Where is she?" she demanded again. "I want to see her."

"Julie," Dr. Daniels said, "why don't you go with Nurse Fleming and sit down for a few moments? I know this is the most shocking news you could receive."

"You must have taken her somewhere."

Julie felt Matt fold his arms around her. "Julie," he said, his voice cracking. "Julie, Julie." He rocked back and forth, repeating her name.

Julie shrugged out of his grief-drenched embrace. "Matt, I have to see her. Please. Please." She turned toward Dr. Daniels and Nurse Fleming. "Let me see her. Once more," she added. "One last time." She felt the first stab of unbearable pain rip into her.

The doctor and the nurse looked at each other and exchanged a wordless dialogue. Dr. Daniels raised a questioning eyebrow. Nurse Fleming nodded.

"Yes, I understand that you need to say good-bye," Dr. Daniels said gently.

The pain swelled. *Good-bye.* A sob of grief rose to Julie's lips. The long tunnel was collapsing. The reality of the doctor's words was taking hold of Julie's heart. She turned back to Matt. His eyes were wet and wide with hurt. "Oh, Matt," she whispered.

He reached for her again, and this time she drew him to her. *Danielle.* Matt's baby, too. Matt's little girl. She felt him break into gasping, silent sobs. But she couldn't cry. Not yet. She held him. *Danielle.*

Her own tearless agony twisted any sense of time. *I have to say good-bye to Danielle. My baby, Danielle.* She held Matt for maybe a moment, maybe far longer. Eventually Matt's body stopped shaking. Eventually he pulled back just enough so she could see his tear-stained face.

"I need to see her, too," he whispered.

Dr. Daniels and Nurse Fleming were now talking quietly. Nurse Fleming nodded and disappeared into the nursery and the back room. Dr. Daniels approached Matt and Julie.

"We'd like to see her," Matt said. "We'd both like to see her."

The doctor nodded. "If you're sure."

Julie considered walking away and never seeing Danielle again. Every nerve in her being went tense with resistance. "Yes, we're sure." She heard her own fierceness.

Dr. Daniels led Julie and Matt through the door to the nursery, past the other nurse on duty, toward the back room. Julie's feet seemed to move as if on remote pilot. Danielle. She was going to see Danielle. For the last time. She felt hollow, weak.

She had a flash of the moment, three years ago, when she'd found out her sister was dead. Disbelief. Shock. Julie felt herself stumble. Matt's arm was immediately under her elbow, steadying her.

Dr. Daniels let them into a small, well-lit laboratory. Nurse Fleming stood back from a bassinet, like the ones the healthy newborns were placed in in the regular nursery. Healthy babies. Living babies. Julie steeled herself. She stepped forward and peered down at Danielle, lying under a white blanket. She looked no different than if she were sleeping peacefully.

Julie didn't know quite what she'd expected to see. Except for the pallor of Danielle's face—not a trace of pink in her cheeks—she looked as if she would wake up any second and smile the smile Julie had gotten to know so well.

Julie was helpless with love and agony. She felt herself drawing nearer to the crib, already leaning down. She had never been this close to her daughter without Plexiglas walls, tubes, latex gloves.

Danielle. My daughter. Julie felt the first silent tear trickle down her face. She reached out her hand and touched Danielle's cheek. It was still warm. All the love she'd ever felt, every invisible bit of her soul seemed to rush toward the spot where her fingers felt her daughter's soft, soft face, flesh on flesh for the very first time. Oh, my God, she would never open her eyes again. Never. She'd never laugh. Never take her first step. Never say her first word.

Julie felt a searing anguish wrench her body. She collapsed over Danielle's tiny, lifeless form, hugging her, warming her with her own tears.

"Julie," Matt said.

Julie looked back over her shoulder at him. Tears were streaming down his cheeks. He was reaching his hand out toward her—toward her and Danielle. "Matt, I just want to hold her. Just once." Her gaze shifted to Dr. Daniels and Nurse Fleming, standing a respectful distance behind Matt.

The doctor nodded.

As Matt moved to Julie's side, she reached under the blanket and pulled it back. She let her hands move over every part of her baby, her round little legs, her perfect toes, her tummy . . . Danielle was unbearably soft, but already stiff with the departure of life from her body.

Gently, Julie lifted Danielle up to her breast. Her daughter's last breath already expired, she held her baby in her arms for the first time.

Sixteen

❧

"It's all my fault." Matt couldn't even lift his head to look at the coffin. "I'm sorry, Danielle. I'm sorry."

One last look. Last chance to see your little girl.

Slowly, fearfully, he picked up his head to look. But as he did, the lid to the coffin slammed shut, right before his eyes. There was a pounding on the wooden box from inside. She was gasping for breath. Matt reached for the lid and tried to pry it open, but it wouldn't budge. The pounding grew louder, and there were shrieks and cries for help. Then it all stopped—silence—and Matt knew he'd never see her again.

He awoke in a puddle of sweat. His heart pounded. He felt a shiver running from head to toe.

This made the third time tonight his nightmare had woken him up. The bedroom was dark and cold. Matt looked over at Julie. She was buried under the covers, in the midst of a deep sleep. On the night table next to her, illuminated by the faint red glow of the alarm-clock light, sat two pill bottles, their caps off. Matt knew they were Julie's only way of getting sleep.

He flipped onto his back and stared into the semidarkness, trying to figure out how he could possibly start to put the pieces of his life back together again. He struggled under a tidal wave of anguish. The accident never would have happened if he hadn't kept holding out on trading in his motorcycle for a car. Keeping the bike was like clinging to the child in him, refusing to grow up. How could he have expected to be a father when he was too irresponsible even to part with his bike?

And that was only part of it. Then he'd made the decision to have Danielle delivered right after the accident. He never should have listened to Dr. Daniels that day. She'd seemed so certain. But now Matt wondered if everything might have been fine if he'd decided not to let them force the birth. Julie's injuries had turned out to be less serious than they'd originally thought. If they'd known, maybe Danielle would have still been safe inside Julie's womb right this moment, the joyous day of her birth still in the future. Why had Matt signed that paper agreeing to Danielle's delivery? Why hadn't he insisted on waiting and letting nature take its course?

Matt tried to push all the miserable questions out of his head. What was done was done. Or, as Julie's father had said, no amount of feeling guilty was going to bring Danielle back to life. Matt needed his strength to go on with his own life—and to help Julie go on with hers.

But images of Danielle haunted his every thought. That first smile she'd given him—a smile that looked so much like Julie's. Would Julie ever smile that way again? And then the day Julie had held Danielle in her arms—Danielle's short life already gone from her body. Matt swallowed back a sob. Over. Her life was over. Three weeks and a day, without even a moment outside that glass room.

The first signs of daylight were visible out the bedroom window. Matt could see the trees on the Town Green across the street, swaying in a fierce fall wind. Today would be cold and gray, appropriate weather for a day that would be devoid of joy. In just a few hours, he and Julie would dress in black to bury their baby.

"Danielle?" Julie cried out in her sleep—

searching, needing, unable to find her. "Danielle?" She rolled over on her side. She freed her arms from under the covers and reached out into the faint, early-morning light. Matt saw her eyes open for a second, flicker, and then shut again, as her arms dropped and she fell back asleep.

Awake or asleep, he feared for Julie. Asleep, the dark was filled with nightmares. Awake, she'd be fraught with panic and tears. When she couldn't stand the pain, she'd reach for a sedative. It would calm her down briefly, let her fall asleep again, but nothing could completely dull the hurt. Hurt that Matt had caused.

Julie hadn't actually come out and accused him. But she'd barely had a chance. In the two days since Danielle's death, they'd been surrounded almost constantly by concerned friends and relatives—Julie's family, Matt's father, Nick, Dahlia . . . Julie wouldn't even talk about Danielle. When anyone mentioned her name, Julie would go silent, pulling all her pain and anger into herself like a snail withdrawing into its shell. And Matt was sure she was eyeing his motorcycle with pure venom—as if Danielle's death were the fault of the shiny steel machine. What could he do to win back her trust? To reforge the bond of love between them? Surely there had to be a way.

He thought about the very beginning of

their relationship. That had begun with a tragedy, too. In a split second of shattering glass and metal, Matt had lost his best friend and Julie her only sister. After the accident, Matt had paid a condolence call on Mark's family, and then on Mary Beth's, even though they were feuding with his father. The Millers hadn't made it easy. But Matt and Julie and Tommy had wound up sitting out in the backyard, telling funny stories about Mary Beth and Mark.

Matt and Julie knew each other slightly before the accident, but they'd never really sat down and talked before that day. Even then, he'd thought she was really pretty, her thick brown hair framing a round face with strong features. He'd liked her broad smile, even though it was bittersweet with memories of her sister. But what he'd noticed most was the way her large brown eyes studied everything so intently—studied and understood.

Remembering that now, Matt was overcome with love for Julie. He wanted to gather her in his arms, kiss away all the misery. But Julie was off in her own, agonized world. She didn't want to let him in.

Back when they'd first met, it had helped to share their grief, to hug away each other's tears. They'd made each other laugh, too.

They'd healed through talking, listening, and sharing, not by burying what had happened. And little by little, they'd fallen in love.

But there was one huge difference between then and now. Matt wasn't responsible for what had happened to Mary Beth and Mark. Julie's accident was another story—a selfish, shameful story that could have been avoided. Could have and should have. Matt threw off the covers and got out of bed. Danielle was being buried today. Would he and Julie ever be able to share anything again?

Silence. Cold silence from Nick as he and Dahlia moved around the room getting dressed, stiffly avoiding each other's gaze. Dahlia cut a wide path around him as she went over to the closet and riffled through her wardrobe. The black knit dress with the buttons up one side? She touched her hand to the hanger. No. Right color, but it was way too short. It would look frivolous, as if she was dressed for a party. The charcoal gray skirt with the matching blazer? Too much like she was applying for an office job.

Darn! What did it matter, anyway? What difference did it make what she wore to Julie's baby's funeral? She yanked the charcoal-colored suit out of the closet and flung it on the bed, flopping down after it. It was her own fault that Danielle was being buried today. Her own lazy, careless fault. She wished Daddy had never given her that fancy car for her high-school graduation—that he'd given her a word processor, or a pen set, or one of those things that regular parents gave their kids.

Dahlia let out a bitter laugh. Yeah, if she'd gotten a gold-plated pen for graduation, Matt and Julie's baby would still be snuggled inside Julie's womb, waiting for the right time to come out into the world.

Dahlia pictured little Danielle as she'd seen her on a visit to the hospital, her face a funny combination of Julie's and Matt's, her mop of brown hair in which one of the nurses had tied a white satin bow, her smile so sweet and angelic, despite the confines of her incubator and the tubes and needles running from her tiny body.

"It's not fair!" Dahlia muttered under her breath. "It's just not fair."

Nick turned to look at her, one arm in the jacket of his suit. "Is something wrong?" he asked tersely.

Dahlia made a face of disbelief. "Is something wrong? We're going to watch them put our friends' baby into the ground and it's my fault and you want to know if something's wrong?"

Nick clicked his tongue. "I meant, like—it

sounded as if maybe your zipper was broken, or your tights had a run, or something." He finished putting on his jacket and gave a tug at the bottom of it to straighten it out. "And anyway, Dahlia, it's *not* your fault. It was an accident. An accident, okay?"

He sounded so angry, so annoyed. Dahlia felt her chest and throat grow tight. "Well, you sure don't make it sound like you believe that."

Nick clicked his tongue again as he picked up his tie from the top of his bureau. "Look, it's a tense time for both of us," he said curtly.

Dahlia watched him slip the tie under the collar of his shirt and loop the long end around the short end. She'd never seen Nick in a suit before, and he looked gorgeous—especially with his cowboy boots for a personal touch. But he was so far away from her, so untouchable.

"You're really furious about this whole Italy thing, aren't you?" she said.

Nick's response was to set his mouth.

Dahlia felt her own anger flare. "I don't know how you can even be thinking about that at a time like this."

Nick gave a short shrug. "Look, if you're trying to say that I don't care about Matt and Julie as much as you do, you're wrong."

"I'm not saying that."

"Then what *are* you saying?" The room seemed to vibrate with tension.

"I'm saying that you're totally jealous that I got into the Rome Institute. That you can't stand it that maybe my essays were better than yours, that they wanted me more." Dahlia knew her words were coming out hard, but Nick had been freezing her out day after day, ever since they'd heard from the institute. It wasn't her fault they'd decided the way they had. But living with Nick was like living with an iceberg.

Nick's jaw was clenched. "Look, Dahlia, if you want to think it's jealousy, fine. But I think you owe me an answer. Are you going, or are you staying?"

Dahlia felt all the pros and cons warring in her head. If she went: the thrill, the art, the language, the new people, the experience she might never have again. If she stayed . . . She glanced around the room. Her gaze fell on the photo of her and Nick in the Painted Desert. She felt her anger give way a little. She looked up at him. If she stayed . . .

But his face was so unyielding, his lean body so tight under his well-tailored suit. He came toward her and sat down, but at the very edge of the bed, carefully, as if he were afraid they might accidentally touch each other.

Dahlia wanted to wrap her arms around him. She needed him so badly. She couldn't shake the picture in her mind of tiny Danielle, nor the heart-wrenching pain of what Julie and Matt had to be feeling right now. The squeal of her faulty brakes echoed in her mind. She needed to be swallowed up in Nick's embrace, to forget about everything for the moment, to let out all the tears that were dammed up inside her. But she held back.

"Look," Nick said. "You know, when something like this happens—something so—so tragic, you realize how important it is to have real support from the people who are most important to you."

Dahlia nodded. Right. Like they needed to hug each other. Maybe she and Nick weren't on such different wavelengths after all. She moved closer to him. His frown stopped her cold.

"I just don't feel like I have that from you right now," he went on. "I don't even know if you're going to be around a couple of months from now."

Dahlia felt a riptide of frustration course through her. Italy. It was all Nick could think about. It was all he kept coming back to. Now. When Julie's baby was about to be laid to rest. "Nick, don't you think you can give it a break today?" she snapped. Then she softened her tone. "I need you, Nick. But when you act like this, it almost makes me think my parents are right about us living together."

"Well, maybe they are."

Dahlia felt a stab of hurt. Nick was supposed to tell her all the reasons her parents were wrong, to hold her and tell her why they were such a good couple, to whisper how much he wanted her to stay in Madison. And she'd say yes. Yes, you mean more to me than all the masterpieces of Italy.

But Nick had gotten up and was straightening his tie. "You'd better hurry and get dressed," he said.

As she put her suit on, there was silence in the room again.

Seventeen

❧

The tiny polished wood casket, not much larger than a bread box, sat on the ground next to the newly dug grave. Julie stared dully at the fresh, raw hole in the earth, and at the little box. Could this really be all that was left of the life she'd carried inside her for all those months? All that was left of the infant she'd rushed to see every day, touching her tenderly through the sterile gloves and dreaming of the day she'd bring her home? Dreaming of bathing her soft, chubby little body in the blue plastic washtub, dreaming of singing to her, dreaming of watching her take her first, shaky-legged step.

Julie swallowed hard. That's all they had been—dreams. Now she'd never know the joy of caring for Danielle, never know the feel of her warm little body, never feel love and joy for her—only love and emptiness, love and unbearable sorrow.

A tear trickled down Julie's cheek and mingled with the fine, cold rain that misted her face. She felt as if she would never get warm again, that no laughter would ever fill the chilling emptiness inside her.

Next to her, Matt stood with his arm touching her shoulder. Julie could feel his body trembling as he sobbed silently. Around the mud-soaked grave, all their relatives and friends were gathered with somber faces. Jerry Collins flanked his son on the other side, arms crossed in front of him, head lowered. Julie's father stood at the head of the grave, a Bible open in his hands.

". . . for an innocent soul who was taken from us before her time . . ." he intoned, his well-practiced preacher's voice made shaky by grief. He looked older than Julie had ever seen him looking, as if years had passed rather than weeks since her family had last come out to Ohio, after the accident. Or was it her own sense that she would never feel young again? Julie wondered. That Danielle's death had taken away part of her life.

Julie's mother's face was pale under the black scarf she'd wrapped around her head, her eyes swollen with crying. She seemed to sway from side to side, bolstered between Julie's father and Tommy. Tommy clutched the worn teddy bear Julie hadn't seen in a very long time.

Snaggles, she thought, the stuffed animal's name popping into her head. Tommy had held Snaggles at Mary Beth's funeral, too. Julie felt a sharp stab of grief. She turned away from her family, unable to take their misery on top of her own.

Julie tried to find solace in the presence of her friends, but their pained expressions only drove home the awful reason they were all gathered together. Dahlia's tears streamed down her cheeks, her blond hair hanging wet and limp from rain. Nick stood at a slight distance from her, his face grim and tense. Marion sobbed openly—leaning against Bailey Smith for support. Julie couldn't even find the strength to feel surprised about that. As she let her gaze wander through the cluster of mourners around Danielle's grave, she noticed Fred standing at the edge of the crowd, his Cincinnati cap held respectfully in his hands.

"Julie, Matthew, those who have gathered here today are your pillar in your time of need," her father was saying. "Find strength in us."

Julie listened to the words but felt no comfort. It was true that much of the community of Madison had come out in the rain to pay their respects. Everyone from Paul and Maya and the gang from Julie's old dorm to locals who Julie recognized from the Barn and Grill. Several of her professors were even in the crowd. But all Julie could feel was the deep well of communal grief. These people should never have had to be gathered together this way.

She remembered the last moments before the accident—the heady freedom of driving in the sporty car, the wind in her hair, the thrill of speed . . . Speed. Julie was consumed with fury at herself. She'd been going way too fast, and she'd known it even at the time. The most precious cargo on board, and she'd been driving like a teenager on a joyride. If she'd been more in control, maybe she could have coasted to safety when the brakes had given out.

And if she hadn't been driving that car at all . . . She worked to shut out a flash of anger at Matt and at Dahlia. Nothing was going to bring Danielle back.

"For she has gone to a better place," Julie's father was now concluding. "Rest in peace, our little Danielle."

A staggered chorus of "amens" sent Danielle on her final journey. Julie worked her mouth, but no sound came out. *A better place,* she echoed silently to herself. *A place where Mary Beth will be waiting for her.* But far from comforting Julie, the thought just seemed to compound the agony of losing them both. She wrapped her arms around herself, unable to stop shivering.

There was a moment of total silence, every person in the crowd immobile with sadness. Then, little by little, there was movement among the mourners, and the sound of soft voices dampened by rain. People began to turn away from the grave.

Two workers in dark green uniforms stepped toward Danielle's casket. Julie flinched as they lifted it, prepared to lower it into the earth. An indescribable agony ripped through her.

"No!" she sobbed. They couldn't put her baby down into the cold, wet ground.

Tommy rushed forward and placed Snaggles on the coffin. "Keep her company," he said, crying.

Julie thought her heart was going to crack on the spot. She twisted away, burying her face in Matt's chest.

His arms went around her and held her tightly. "It's okay, it's okay," he repeated. "Okay, Julie."

But his words were just empty sounds. Julie

could feel Matt's body, trembling out of control. Danielle was gone. A few brief weeks in her incubator and her life was over. Julie knew nothing would ever be okay again.

It seemed strangely like a party. The apartment was filled with noise, warmth, food, and lots of familiar faces. Matt sat on a straight chair and surveyed the odd collection of people. Friends from Julie's old dorm, people from the Barn and Grill, professors. Dr. Zinn, the man who'd cured Matt of cancer, was there. He was sitting on the couch, talking with Julie's mother. Jane Moore, Julie's editor from the newspaper, was helping herself to a piece of cake. Paul and Maya were there, arm in arm to comfort each other.

They'd all come to pay their respects, to be there with Matt and Julie, to help ease the pain. And in fact, the sound of familiar voices, the sight of a smile, even an occasional laugh seemed to help cushion the ache. Matt was never alone long enough to sink into the memories and the despair he knew were waiting for him.

He felt a comforting hand on his shoulder. "Hanging in there?"

"Pat, hi." She was still dressed in black from the funeral. "Yeah, I suppose. Just barely."

"Aren't you going to eat? It doesn't look like you touched a thing."

Matt looked down at the plate full of food he was holding in his hand. Roast beef, baked lasagna, potato salad, a mound of coleslaw, cranberry sauce. He didn't remember ever being given the food. Who'd handed it to him? Mrs. Miller? Nick? Or had Pat just placed it in his hand a moment ago? "I didn't even realize I was holding this. I know it sounds awfully weird, but—"

"But you've had a pretty rough day," Pat said. "Hey, it's all right."

Matt swallowed hard. He could feel the bitter agony of his loss lying in wait for him, like a wild animal waiting to pounce.

"I have an idea of how you're feeling, Matt." Pat spoke softly, gently. "Empty. Terrified. A little weirded out by all the people who've poured in here."

Matt nodded. She knew exactly how he felt. "A lot weirded out, actually."

"I know. I was where you are now—after my brother died."

"Your brother?" He looked up at her. "You never told me about—"

"Alexander. Yeah, he was the best. I don't know, it's not something I love talking about. It was a long time ago. I was nine years old. He was fifteen. Stubborn. He was the most stubborn kid in the world. In the middle of March, he decided to go skating. 'The pond's still frozen,' he swore. Nobody paid much attention to him when he grabbed his skates and headed for the pond. Alone." She shrugged. Her hand tugged at a lock of blond hair. "The fire department fished him out the next morning. Sometimes I still can't believe it really happened."

Matt barely knew what to say. "I'm sorry, Pat."

"Yeah. Anyway," she continued, "the next thing I knew, he was dead and buried and there were a million people in our house. Just like there are here. And the food! Aunt Sophie made her famous lemon cake. Our next-door neighbors brought a tuna casserole. Alex's teacher brought Jell-O molds and cranberry sauce."

"Just like today. The big party," Matt said.

"You got it," she said. "Everybody was talking and laughing. Laughing, that was the strangest part of it. Alex had just died, and people were laughing and eating. I really thought I was the only one who cared. Until my cousin Jeff forced a few bites of tuna casserole on me, I hadn't realized how hungry I was. And how much better eating made me feel."

"Come to think of it, Pat," Matt said, glancing at the plate of food in his hand. "Maybe I am a little hungry. I mean, my stomach's hungry, but I don't really feel like eating at all. I don't think I have the right to. I mean—"

Pat put her hand on Matt's shoulder. "Try it. It just might help you keep going during the worst times. And that plate of food looks a heck of lot better than that tuna casserole did."

Matt managed a weak smile. "Okay, I'll eat." As soon as the first forkful of lasagna entered his mouth, he realized that he was starved. "Hey, it's delicious. I feel like it's the first bite of food I've had in a year."

Pat smiled. "Marcy's secret recipe."

"Marcy? She can cook?" Over at the other end of the room, Marcy was talking to Bailey Smith. Somehow, Matt couldn't picture her in the kitchen.

"Not the homemaker type, huh?" Pat asked, following Matt's gaze.

Matt was surprised at the sound of his own laughter. Pat smiled. "You're a real friend, Pat," Matt said.

"Thanks," she said. "You know I'm here for you guys. We all are."

Matt took a bite of potato salad and looked around. Gwen and Sarah Pike were filling up their glasses with soda. Scott and Bob were talking to Julie's friend John Graham. Leon and

Nick stood at either side of Julie's father. The Reverend looked so odd dressed in black, sitting in the leopard-print chair.

"See that guy over there with Julie's brother?" Matt pointed to Professor Copeland, Julie's journalism professor from the year before. Tommy was showing the stocky, bearded professor how to play his hand-held video game. Professor Copeland was wide-eyed with intrigue as Tommy gave the demonstration. "Hard to believe that man is the most feared teacher in the whole school," Matt said.

"Don't I know it." Pat laughed. "He put an end to my hopes of being a journalist."

Chitchat, warmth, and lots of food. It was comforting to know that it would go on all afternoon. During the saddest time in his life, Matt knew he was lucky having so many people there to help him through it. This morning, he'd thought he'd never breathe again, never smile. Now he was starting to see that there was hope. Human contact meant everything.

Take advantage of it while they're all here, he thought to himself. Matt knew the clock was ticking. Soon enough the guests would leave and he'd relive the horror. He shivered. He was afraid of getting into bed and having to face another night of bad dreams. He was afraid of Julie's silence.

He spotted Julie by the living-room window. She had her arms wrapped tightly around Dahlia. Julie's back was to Matt, but he knew she was crying. As Dahlia hugged her, she patted the back of Julie's head, trying to calm her down.

Julie had barely been able to speak during the funeral. She'd barely looked at Matt all day. When Tommy had tossed his stuffed bear into the grave, Matt could practically see Julie's heart shattering into even more pieces. When the gravediggers lowered Danielle's casket into the ground, she'd refused to look.

"How about seconds? Let me fill up your plate, huh?"

Matt saw Pat reaching out to take his plate. "Huh?" Her voice took him by surprise. It wasn't the first time today he'd blanked out, slipped back into his cocoon of unbearable sorrow. "Yeah, sure. Thanks."

As Pat walked away, Matt closed his eyes and listened to the sound of so many voices. *Take comfort in it now,* he told himself. Because in a little while, the party would be over and he and Julie would be alone. More alone than they'd ever been in their lives.

Eighteen

❧

Julie sat in the leopard-print armchair, her gaze fixed on the part of the room where Danielle's nursery had been set up. Matt and Nick had taken the child-size furniture down to the basement of Secondhand Rose and pushed the sofa and the rest of the living-room furniture back to their usual spots. But in her mind's eye, Julie could still see Danielle's little wooden crib, the fish mobile fluttering above it, the changing table, the little chest of drawers.

Julie's stomach was hollow, but she had no appetite. She'd cried so many tears she wasn't sure she had any left. All she felt was a boundless emptiness, no less today than it had been yesterday or the day before.

Meanwhile, the parade of visitors had trickled away. Everyone had finally gone back to their lives—to work, to school. Even Mom and Dad and Tommy had gone back to Philadelphia a few days after the funeral. Julie's friends were still calling to check in, or dropping by between classes, but less frequently. In the week since Danielle's funeral, Julie found herself alone more and more often. Thoroughly alone. All she could find to console herself were her thoughts of how it could have been: teaching her little pink-cheeked toddler to say "Mama" and "Dada"; sitting Danielle on her knee and reading her the books Julie remembered best from her own childhood; splashing around in the quarry with her on a hot summer day . . .

The sound of Matt's footsteps on the stairs and his key in the door didn't make her feel any less lonely. As hard as Matt was trying to make her feel better, his own pain was so clear that it only made hers worse. She steeled herself as he walked into the apartment.

"Hi, sweetheart," he said with false brightness.

Why? Why even bother to try? Julie thought. His smile was pasted on, wax-paper transparent, his sorrow showing right through it.

"How are you?" he asked, taking a few steps toward her.

Julie shrugged, responding with a question

of her own rather than answering his. "How was class?"

"Fine," Matt said softly.

"Oh." What difference did it make? Fine. Not so fine. It was just a class—a bunch of books, some lectures, a few tests. It wasn't life. Or death.

Matt came over and dropped to a squat in front of her. "You didn't go back to school today?"

Julie avoided his gaze. She shook her head.

"And what about work?"

"Jane told me I could take some time off. They all understand."

Matt frowned. "Julie, I'm sure they do, but I'm *not* sure it's the best thing for you." He reached out and put a hand on her knee. Julie felt the weight of it. She didn't pull back, but she didn't respond, either. She couldn't. "You've got to do something," Matt went on, gently but insistently. "Get out of the house, get some fresh air. It's a pretty nice day out. We could take a walk. You're healed up enough now."

Julie felt the corners of her mouth turn down. "I got out," she said, hearing her voice rise on a defensive note. "I went to the park earlier today," she added.

She pictured Danielle's tiny grave site, the squares of sod that had been laid over the raw earth just beginning to grow together in a seamless blanket of grass. Soon there would be a small slate headstone proclaiming her too-short time on earth. *Beloved daughter of Julie and Matt,* it would say beneath the dates. Her father had suggested a poem by the poet Robert Bridges to be carved beneath that: *Perfect little body, without fault or stain on thee.* Julie wondered how there would be enough space on the little stone for all the words.

"The park," Matt said sadly. Julie could see he knew where she'd been. "Look, maybe we should get away from here," he said. "Go away for a week or two, get a change of scenery. I'm sure I could arrange some time off at work, and some makeup assignments from Professor Clark."

Julie felt a well of resistance. She shook her head hard. *Beloved daughter.* "I can't leave her," she said.

"Julie," Matt said, his voice almost a whisper, "she's gone. *She's* left *us.* We can't change that."

Julie wanted to cover her ears with her hands, blot out his words. Of course it was true, but hearing him say it out loud only sharpened her pain.

"You think it's my fault, don't you?" Matt asked.

She studied Matt's unhappy face. Was it his fault? Her own? She pressed her lips together. Did it really make a difference? *Beloved daughter.* Three weeks on earth. "Matt, I don't hold you responsible," she said weakly.

"You don't?" Matt sounded doubtful.

Julie shrugged. Maybe she did. What did it matter?

Matt sank down cross-legged on the floor in front of her. "I couldn't bear for you to hate me with our anniversary coming up," he said. "It's next week, you know. Our first anniversary."

Julie felt a spark of surprise. Their anniversary? But the spark went out almost immediately. Their first anniversary, and she felt no joy at all. If she and Matt hadn't married, she would never have known the grief of Danielle's death.

"Maybe we should go on a special trip," Matt went on. "Maybe take the honeymoon we didn't get last year. Skiing in the Rockies? Lying on the beach in Mexico? It's not like we have much money, but I'll figure out something." He sighed. "Julie, I know how much you hurt. You know I do, don't you?"

Julie raised her shoulders. How could he know? He hadn't felt Danielle moving inside him as she blossomed with life. He hadn't had the morning sickness, the swollen belly, the aches and pains that reminded her every hour of every day that a new life was forming in her. And he hadn't been the one driving so free and carelessly down the highway before the accident that had taken Danielle's life. He didn't see it in his mind day after unbearable day: the highway divider looming up crazily, the moment of impact that had taken their baby's life.

Matt swallowed hard. "Julie, I *do* understand. I feel all the pain you feel. I really had to force myself to get out of bed this morning—to leave the house and get myself to class. But you know what? I felt a little better when I did." He gave a sad laugh. "I'm not going to tell you I had a good day. I've never hurt like this, Jules. But we can't give up on life."

He paused, caught in some kind of reflection. "Remember after Mary Beth and Mark died? We thought we'd never be happy again. And maybe we even felt a little weird the first time we really laughed and went out and had fun. But it really was good to feel alive again, you know? To discover that the world was still out there. That the stars were still out there."

Julie knew exactly what he was remembering—that time after the movies in the parking lot outside the theater in Philly, when the stars had been so perfect against the velvet sky and they had shared their first kiss. But through the veil of her grief, the memory seemed impossibly distant, too long ago for Julie to get a grasp on how she'd felt.

"Don't give up, Julie," Matt said, urgency creeping into his voice. "It won't bring Danielle back. Your father told me that, and he's right."

Julie heard the truth in Matt's words, but she couldn't help the pure emptiness that she felt. She wished she could have died instead of Danielle.

"Look, when I first came up with the big roommate-exchange plan, you were all afraid you were rushing into living with Nick, right?" Paul Chase asked, adding a dollop of milk to his mug of mocha java. He and Dahlia were seated at a back table of DeCaf, Madison College's own coffeehouse. About half of the dozen or so tiny, round, candlelit tables were occupied, and up on DeCaf's small stage a round-faced girl with a squeaky voice sang folk songs and strummed an acoustic guitar.

Dahlia nodded. "Right. So?" She broke off a piece of a giant chocolate-chip cookie, still warm from the DeCaf oven, and popped it into her mouth.

"So now you want to rush *out* of living with him," Paul said. He leaned forward so he could be heard above the music. The musician had a fan club up at some of the front tables, singing along with her. "You love him, remember?" Paul reminded Dahlia. "You've got to try and work it out."

"You're just saying that because you and Maya don't want to trade back rooms," Dahlia said.

Paul grinned. "Well, okay. That, too," he admitted.

Dahlia pushed away the cookie plate and sighed. She felt a rush of envy at Paul's lovesick expression. She and Nick had looked that way—and not too long ago, either. What had happened, she wondered miserably. "It's such a mess," she said to Paul.

Paul's grin melted into a sympathetic shake of his head. He ran a hand through his mess of wild brown curls. "Sussman with boy troubles."

"Mega boy troubles," Dahlia confirmed. "He sleeps all the way over on the edge of his side of the bed, and by the time I wake up, he's already dressed and out of there." She felt a stab of hurt as she thought about this morning— opening one sleepy eye just in time to see Nick's lean, jean-clad figure slipping out of the door. It was like the bad old days when Dahlia had spent every day dreaming about a few nice words from Nick, or a smile that would never come. And now she was faced with his coldness first thing every morning and last thing every night.

"And it's all about whether you go to Italy or not?" Paul asked. "Man, I wish they'd turn down the volume on this tofu music," he added. "Now, if they'd play some real rock and roll around this place . . ."

Dahlia found herself laughing in spite of her mood. When it came to old friends, she could always count on Paul—from sharing his pail and shovel in the sandbox a gazillion years ago to listening to her problems now. She toyed with the soft wax dripping down the side of the candle on their table. "It's not just about whether I go. It's about the fact that I got into the program and he didn't. You know, he's supposed to be the smart one." She felt the familiar anger course through her.

"Yeah? Dahlia, anyone who grew up listening to your homework excuses knows how smart you are. An A-plus for creativity, too. 'Oh, my mother took me to a benefit at the Alliance Française this weekend, and I brought my French notebook with me. You know, I thought I might find someone who'd give me a little extra help with the subjunctive. Well, somehow it wound up in a puddle of *potage aux légumes*. Oh, I'm so sorry, Madame Vericourt . . .'"

Dahlia giggled. "No, I didn't really say that!"

Paul nodded. "Yup. And a perfect French accent on the *potage aux légumes*. Just for a little flavor *français*. I don't think she ever believed you, but you sure kept her *très amusée*."

Dahlia sighed. "Which is more than I seem to do for Nick these days. The thing is, it's like, why should I stick around when he's acting so awful? He deserves for me to go off and find some tall, dark, and handsome Italian boyfriend."

"And at the same time, you think maybe if you tell him you're sticking around, he'll thaw out a little," Paul said.

Dahlia nodded. "I don't know. It's like the opportunity of a lifetime. You'd think if the guy really loved me, he'd want me to have it. I mean, if we're right for each other, we ought to be able to get through a semester apart, right?" As she said the words, Dahlia felt a tickle of reminiscence. She gave a little laugh. "Yeah, that's what Julie said about her and Matt at the beginning of school last year."

Paul sipped his coffee. "Hey, maybe that means if you go to Rome, Nick will show up and whisk you off to get married. Romantic honeymoon driving one of those toy-size cars all over Italy? Not too shabby, Sussman."

"Right. In my dreams," Dahlia said. But she couldn't help imagining her and Nick in a tiny Fiat Toppolino, decorated with tin cans and streamers and a "Just Married" sign, climbing a switchback road up a mountain toward some medieval castle where they were to spend their wedding night.

"Hey," Paul said, his tone turning serious. "How are they doing, anyway? Julie and Matt. I called the other day, but no one was there."

Dahlia felt her own problems suddenly dwarfed by worry over her friends. "Or else Julie was there and she was refusing to pick up the phone. I think she just hangs out and stares at the walls all day. Yesterday I went over there and she was just sitting in the living room not doing anything. She didn't even have the TV or radio on. I tried to cheer her up, but forget it."

Dahlia felt a sting of frustration all over again. "I mean, she *says* she doesn't blame me for what happened, but I don't really believe her. She's so miserable, and so angry. That's the other thing about going to Italy. How can I cut out on Julie and Matt at a time like this?"

"So you're thinking of staying, but you want to move out on Nick?" Paul said. "That seems like the worst idea. Then you don't have him *or* your trip to Italy. Plus, you tear me away from the woman I love," he added melodramatically. He put his hand over his heart.

"Save it, Chase," Dahlia said. "Anyway, aside from what's going on between me and Nick, my folks seem to be hot on the trail of the roommate exchange. That could be the end of it for all of us. Especially if they get wise enough to talk to dear old Doreen, the dorm coordinator."

Paul's mouth turned down in a deep frown. "Bummer," he said. "Then maybe you better get on that plane to Rome right away. Before our cover's blown."

Dahlia shot him a look.

"Kidding. Just kidding," he said. "We'll all miss you if you go. You know that."

Dahlia felt a flush of warmth. Maybe it was corny, but Paul's words made her feel good. She never got the feeling that her parents really missed her, just that they wanted to make sure she was staying in line, behaving as they thought she should. It was nice to be surrounded by people who really seemed to care about her. She'd never had such good friends before.

She and Julie had written and called each other all summer. Maya had sent her two postcards from L.A. Scott had stopped by when he'd come into New York for a big concert at Madison Square Garden. Her friends here were for keeps, unlike her high-school friends. She'd already lost touch with many of them.

But of course, her most important friend here was Nick, or he had been until war had broken out. Dahlia drained her coffee cup. How was she supposed to decide what to do?

Nineteen

❦

"Aren't you even going to have one bite?" Matt asked softly. "It's your favorite. Anniversary delicious."

Julie stared guiltily at the untouched piece of chocolate cheesecake. She knew how hard Matt had worked all afternoon preparing their anniversary dinner. She could feel him studying her from across the table.

She looked up at him. Soft candlelight flickered across his strong, handsome features. She tried to remember the thrill she'd always felt looking into Matt's deep-set gray eyes. As she held his gaze, his sad expression gave way to a glimmer of hope.

But all Julie felt was emptiness. She couldn't seem to touch the love she'd once felt for Matt—or find the appetite she'd once had for life. It wasn't that she didn't want to find it. She just couldn't. Danielle's tiny heart had stopped beating, and Julie felt dead inside, too. She let her gaze fall away from Matt's.

Matt pushed back his chair with a squeak of wood against tile, got up, and began to clear the table. "Well, I'll wrap it all and put it in the fridge. Maybe you'll feel like a midnight snack," he said. He sounded tired, so tired.

Julie knew how much she was hurting him right now—on top of his own pain over Danielle. But somehow, she just couldn't get herself to put her arms around him, kiss his forehead, or whisper that she loved him. She watched his back as he disappeared into the kitchen with the leftover cake and dirty dishes.

When he came out, he was holding a small, gift-wrapped box. "I'll clean up later," he said. "I have something I want to give you." He took Julie by the hand, and she let him lead her into the living room. She felt like a robot, automatically walking after him.

She sat down stiffly on the sofa. Matt sat close by her and offered her the box. "Happy anniversary," he said.

She ran her finger over the red satin bow. "I don't have anything for you," she said. She felt a pinch of selfishness and overwhelming sadness. Her first anniversary, and she had no present for Matt. She hadn't even thought about it. "I'm sorry, Matt."

He shrugged. "It's okay. I understand. Really. Now go ahead and open it. That'll be enough of a present for me."

Julie swallowed hard and nodded. She undid the ribbon, peeling back the striped wrapping paper. Usually she tried to figure out what was inside before she took the lid off a surprise package, but tonight she just didn't have the strength for guessing games.

Inside the small box, on a bed of cotton, lay a silvery marcasite brooch in the shape of a pear. Julie lifted it out of the box.

"Do you like it?" Matt asked anxiously. "It's from Secondhand Rose. Just like our wedding rings," he added.

The brooch was lovely. The tiny metal facets glimmered like jewels in the light that came in from the street lamps through the living-room windows. Julie held the pear-shaped pin in the palm of her hand. "It *is* beautiful," she said, tilting her hand back and forth so the metal sparkled. *Like a big, beautiful, glittering teardrop,* she thought. She felt a tear of her own moisten the corner of her eye.

Matt looked as if he'd been doused with cold water. "I didn't mean my gift to be sad." Matt was trying so hard to make this evening special, and Julie just couldn't respond.

"Oh, Matt, I'm sorry," she said. The tear worked its way down her cheek, followed by another.

Matt took the brooch and box from her and set them on the coffee table. As the tears began to roll down, he drew her to him and enveloped her in a strong hug. "Go ahead. Cry," he whispered. "If it'll make you feel better, cry."

Julie could hear the sob in his own voice. She let go a flood of misery, gasping against his shoulder. *Danielle.* How could she ever celebrate anything after losing her baby daughter?

She cried until there were no more tears left to cry. But she didn't feel better. The big teardrop glistened on the table. No amount of tears was going to bring Danielle back.

"Jewelry, music, candlelight, I even made her favorite dessert—and nothing." Matt tapped the walking stick he'd picked up as he continued up the hill. "Nothing except more tears."

"I wish there was something I could say that would cheer you up," Nick said.

Matt sighed. "Yeah, I know. But there really isn't anything *anybody* can say. I'm glad I've got somebody listening, though. Thanks, Nick."

"Hey, I couldn't very well pass up a hike up Mount Landfill." Mount Landfill was the man-made mountain out behind the gym, built for the cross-country team to practice on when they'd dug the foundations for the new North Campus dorms.

Matt let out a little laugh. He and Julie liked to joke about it being the only hill in the Midwest. "Not much of a hike, huh?"

"I've done steeper," Nick agreed. "But I'm still psyched to get up to the highest point in northwestern Ohio."

"Well, it's not the Rockies, but it is a really beautiful view from the top. You can see the quarry over the edge on the other side."

"Lead on, then," Nick said.

A faraway November sun cast a somber light over the barren fields stretched out around them. The gently sloping rocky path they were on wound its way through patches of spruce and evergreen trees. They walked for a while in silence, the only noise coming from their footsteps on the crunchy leaves and the hollow, rhythmic tapping of Matt's walking stick.

"Maybe you should have taken Julie instead of me, Matt," Nick said. "I mean, if the good food didn't work, maybe some nice scenery could help cheer her up a little."

Matt shrugged. "Nah. It's not like I haven't suggested it. A walk in the woods, a ride on our mountain bikes, anything. But she just doesn't want to cheer up."

"She's really hurting," Nick commented. "Who can blame her?"

"I know. And that's the other half of it. Every time I go out and do something for myself, like hiking with you, I feel as if I shouldn't. Like I should stay home and be depressed."

"Come on," Nick protested. "That's crazy. Why should you do that?"

"Because I *am* depressed," Matt said sharply. "Every minute, I'm thinking about how much I miss Danielle. That beautiful little smile of hers. Every day I hate myself for not having sold the motorcycle and gotten a car. Every day I feel guilty about everything."

"Hey, Matt. You gotta lay off that one," Nick said. "It's not your fault. Just forget it."

"I can't forget it," Matt said. "I feel bad every time I catch myself smiling. I know it's crazy, but I can't help it. I'm out here living life, and my baby never will." He felt a tightness in his chest.

"Hold on a minute," Nick said. "Do you really think Danielle would want you to give up the rest of your happiness and be miserable forever?"

Matt shrugged.

"You already know the answer to that one."

"You mean, like there's no harm in taking a walk or riding your bike? Like if it makes you feel better, why not? Like, isn't that the whole point? To feel better."

"You *do* understand."

"Yeah, sure I do. It's what I tell Julie every day. To try and find a little something that will help make her feel human again." Matt did know how important it was to smile and laugh once in a while. The few times that he'd managed it in the past weeks had helped to make him feel that there was a spark of hope. In the middle of all the desperation and turmoil, it was important to find sanctuary in a moment of laughter or in some other little bit of pleasure. It made all the difference in the world.

If only Julie could realize that. But she was refusing to try. Rather than come along for a hike, she'd stay home in bed. When she went outside, it was to visit the cemetery. "Julie can't laugh," Matt said. "Not yet. Not even for a second. Nothing seems to make her smile. I'm sort of afraid that nothing ever will."

"But you're two different people. Each of you will take different amounts of time to heal."

"Maybe." Matt shrugged. "I guess it's that I

almost lost my chance at life when I was diagnosed with cancer. Now that I've got it back, I'm going to hold on to it—no matter what. But Julie—I just hope that when she comes around, she'll remember how much I love her."

"I bet she will, Matt," Nick said confidently. "She will. If there's one thing I'm certain about, it's that what you and Julie have is real. It'll last. At least one couple will make it," he added under his breath.

"Still trouble in paradise?"

"Paradise?" Nick let out a bitter laugh. "I think you've got the wrong Nick and Dahlia. We left paradise quite a while ago. Paradise disappeared just about when Rome came into view. At least for one of us."

"I guess that means she's going," Matt said.

"Sure. I mean, I suppose she is. I mean—" Nick let out a tremendous sigh. "I don't know what I mean, really. One minute I think she's going, the next she's staying."

"And you don't know where that leaves you."

Nick blew out a long breath. "Bummed. That's where. Sad, angry. This morning she didn't even say hello." He paused, as if remembering the moment. "Then again, I suppose I wasn't my most pleasant self, either. All I know is that it'll be a relief when next semester comes and she heads off to Italy. Dahlia Sussman in Rome. The Colosseum, cappuccino, Italian lovers. It's where she belongs. And once she goes, we won't have to worry about her parents finding out about our living arrangement, either."

"Somehow, I don't believe you really mean what you're saying, Nick," Matt said.

"Well, I don't know. I think the only reason we're still living together is because Paul and Maya are so blissfully in love, we can't separate them long enough to move their stuff out. Look. I'll admit it, I think we have—I mean *had*—a great relationship. I've never met anybody quite like Dahlia. I wish she'd stay and work it out with me. I wish she was the kind of person who'd stay and try, rather than run away, on to the next thing that will occupy her interest for a little while. But—"

"But what?" Matt interrupted. "Careful, Nick. Don't underestimate Dahlia. That girl will surprise you every once in a while." Matt stopped and placed his walking stick on a small patch of earth near the edge of the path. "We're here. The highest point in northwestern Ohio." He speared the stick into the ground for emphasis. Out past a brown cornfield of withered stalks, the quarry glimmered.

"Nice," Nick said. "Maybe it's a good thing

that we're in northwestern Ohio, though," he added, beginning to laugh.

"What do you mean?"

"Well, here we are, totally depressed, as high up as we can get. And the funny thing is, if we were to jump, we probably wouldn't even sprain an ankle."

Twenty

❧

Julie opened her menu, skimmed it without really seeing what was listed, and closed it again. She let it drop on the linen tablecloth. "I'll have whatever you're having," she told Dahlia.

Dahlia frowned. "Julie, how often do you get treated to lunch at the best Italian restaurant in Ohio? There's two whole pages of great dishes to choose from. *Delizioso.* All of it." Dahlia leaned across the table and whispered conspiratorially, "I mean, I know it's not like saying it's the best Italian restaurant in Italy or anything, but still . . ."

Julie knew Dahlia was trying to make her laugh, but she couldn't get herself to respond. Dahlia kept trying. "And hey, it's a pretty good view for the Midwest, don't you think?" Outside, Lake Erie sparkled in the afternoon sun.

"If you use your imagination a little, you can pretend to be on the Mediterranean, huh?"

Julie forced a tight smile. "Yeah, I guess."

"Did I tell you this was where I went on my first date with Nick?"

"About a dozen times." Julie forced a short laugh.

"Oh. I guess the happier days are on my mind," Dahlia said.

Happier days, Julie thought grimly. She could certainly relate to that. She looked around the restaurant. Elegant but simple, with fresh flowers on every table and string-quartet music playing softly from hidden speakers. She noticed a waiter in black trousers and a white shirt approaching the table.

Dahlia patted her menu. "Well, I've known what I wanted since I made the reservation two days ago. How does veal piccata sound? Lemon and butter sauce? Linguine with wild mushrooms on the side, and hot antipasto to start?"

Julie didn't know how she was going to eat a bite. "Fine," she said stiffly.

Dahlia flashed her a big, overdone smile. "Great. You're going to love it."

Julie couldn't help but feel a tickle of irritation. How could Dahlia be so cheerful when Julie was so down? Dahlia would never be able to understand how she was feeling. Dahlia hadn't carried a tiny, living, growing creature around inside her for over half a year. Dahlia hadn't felt a mother's love and a mother's inconsolable grief.

Dahlia turned her smile on the waiter and greeted him in Italian. *"Buon giorno, signorina,"* he responded. "May I take your orders?"

"Si. Un antipasto caldo, due vitelli piccata . . ." Dahlia rattled off the dishes with dramatic flair. As the waiter nodded and headed for the kitchen, Dahlia laughed. "Why go all the way to Rome when I can practice my Italian right in Ohio, huh?"

"Sounded good," Julie said. She heard the listlessness of her own words, but she couldn't help it.

Dahlia's laughter caught in her throat. "Listen," she said quietly. "I can't stand to see you like this. None of your friends can. We love you, Julie—you know that."

The sentiment was nice. Julie wished she could take some real consolation in it, but it was as if her feelings were divorced from anything anyone could say.

"It's been—what? Three weeks? Four weeks?"

"Three." *And two days.*

"Julie, you've got to come back and join the rest of us in the land of the living. I know it hurts incredibly, but we miss you."

I know it hurts. The words echoed in Julie's head. No, Dahlia didn't know. Dahlia couldn't know the depth of Julie's pain. Come back to the land of living? Julie wasn't sure she could. She shrugged.

Dahlia took a deep breath. "Look, Julie, I know you told me you don't blame me for what happened, but you seem so—so cold."

"That's nonsense," Julie said automatically, but she was surprised at the current of anger that was whirling to the surface. If Dahlia had repaired her car . . . If Matt had sold his bike . . . If she'd been driving more carefully . . . There were too many ifs. Maybe they were all responsible.

"Well, if it's nonsense, then why won't you let me in?" Dahlia said.

Julie frowned in annoyance. "Let you in? In where?"

"Julie, you know what I mean. I come over to visit, and it's like I'm talking to a wall. I take you out to lunch, and you act like it's worse than a visit to the dentist." Dahlia laughed wanly at her own joke.

Julie's irritation spiraled. "You know, Dahlia, it's not always about *you*. How I act to *you*. What I think of *you*. There's something else going on right now that's a little more important than *you*."

Dahlia's face crumpled in hurt. "Is that what you think? That I'm only thinking about myself? That I'm taking you to lunch for *me,* that I'm visiting you for *me,* that I call you up all the time so I can talk about *myself*?" Her voice wavered. "Somehow I thought I was showing you I cared. Somehow I thought that friends were supposed to be there for each other. At bad times and good times." Dahlia looked as if she might be about to cry. "But no. It's not about friendship. It's about selfish, self-centered Dahlia. Out for herself. The girl with everything who wants more. You think it, Nick thinks it . . ."

Julie felt chastened. "Look, Dahlia, I'm sorry. You know I didn't mean what I said. I'm just—" She let out a long, noisy sigh. "I guess I'm just feeling so awful."

Dahlia nodded. "You're allowed."

"I don't think you're selfish. I think you're my best friend, okay?"

Dahlia didn't look fully convinced, but she nodded. "Okay."

"Listen, maybe we should just change the subject."

"Sure." Dahlia shrugged. There was a fragile silence at the table. Then Dahlia forced a little laugh. "Hey, guess who I saw making out right in the middle of the cafeteria line at dinner last night?"

She didn't wait for Julie to guess. "Marion—our sweet, innocent Marion—and Bailey Smith! I mean, I knew they were hanging out together, but to actually see them in action—what a trip! I don't know, maybe she learned something about the birds and the bees from growing up with all those animals on the farm or something. They were really going at it. People carrying their trays around them, practically bumping into them, and they were on their own little planet." Dahlia's words tumbled out one on top of another, as if she were trying to cover up the near-explosive moment she and Julie had just had.

Julie nodded. "Yeah, she came over to visit the other day. Total fireworks in her eyes."

"Or somewhere," Dahlia cracked.

Julie managed a little laugh. "I just sort of wonder if they ever talk about anything, you know? Like the way Marion and Fred were always talking about zygotes and quarks and the unification theory, and no one could understand a word they were saying."

Dahlia nodded. "Well, they sure weren't getting much talking done in the cafeteria. I was pretty jealous, I gotta say. Nick hasn't kissed me like that in eons. Hasn't kissed me at all, actually. The guy practically doesn't even talk to me these days, either." She let out a loud sigh.

Julie listened to Dahlia go on about the cold war in her room. She nodded where she was supposed to nod, and shook her head where she was supposed to shake her head. But she couldn't help feeling that Dahlia's problems were small compared to her own. To go to Rome or not. To be mad at Nick or not. If only Julie's problems were like those. Julie's sadness and the angry words she and Dahlia had exchanged hung over the table like an invisible mist.

Out on the lake, a fishing boat moved slowly but steadily, growing smaller and smaller as it headed toward the horizon. Julie wished she could be like the boat, floating away, away, until it disappeared into nothing.

Julie watched from the kitchen table as Matt pulled on his forest-green sweater and hoisted his knapsack onto his back.

Julie flashed him a forced smile. "Well, have a good day."

Matt came over and tilted her chin up so their eyes met. "I'm going to try to," he said seriously. "You try, too. Please, Jules. Do something good for yourself today."

He bent down and kissed her softly on the mouth. Then again. Julie felt a little tug of guilt. She knew how much Matt needed some tiny show of affection. She put her arms around his neck and kissed him back, letting her lips linger on his.

She felt Matt responding, his kiss deepening, his mouth searching hers. She went through all the familiar motions—but she was just acting. When Matt finally pulled away, she felt a breeze of relief.

"Bye," he said softly, giving her a little smile.

Through the open kitchen door, she watched him cross the living room and head out. She knew she was making him hurt. And she wished she could get herself to do something about it. But she couldn't reach out.

As the front door closed behind Matt, she stretched her left hand out in front of her and studied the three silver wedding bands on her ring finger. Past, present, and future. At least that's what they were supposed to represent. It felt more like past, past, past.

The present—well, it was swallowed up in grief, in anger, in memories of the accident, of Danielle. And the future? Danielle was the future, and Danielle was dead. The union of her and Matt was dead.

Julie pushed her chair away from the kitchen table and got up, leaving the dirty breakfast dishes where they were. She remembered when she and Matt had discovered these chairs at a yard sale over on Chestnut Street. They'd been covered with layers of peeling paint and looked as if they'd been in someone's basement for most of the century.

"Uh-uh," Julie had said. But Matt swore he could make them look as good as new.

"Actually, better. Think antique, Julie." And when he'd sanded them and refinished them, he'd been right.

Julie remembered how much they'd laughed, lugging the chairs through half of Madison, stopping to sit down in the middle of Main Street to the stares of all the passersby. Had it been only a year ago? It seemed like another time. Almost as if it had happened to someone else. Someone full of life and plans and hope.

Julie went into the living room. All around her was her life with Matt: the rug that used to be in his room in Philadelphia, the flannel shirt that Julie had given him for his birthday last year, the armchair Dahlia had given them as a wedding present. But everything Julie looked at felt like part of the past—things that had meant something once upon a time.

She made a mental inventory of the contents of the room. The TV, the toaster oven, and a half-dozen other things in the apartment were from Dahlia, too. Julie thought about the day Dahlia had come over with boxes and boxes of stuff piled into her tiny car.

Her car. Julie felt every muscle in her body clench up as she saw the highway divider loom up in her mind's eye. Then the sickening cymbal crash of metal and glass. Her hands went automatically to her belly.

She took a deep breath and tried to calm her racing heart. *The past,* she told herself. The car was the past—the awful, horrific past.

She walked over to the bookshelves and picked up a framed photo of her and Matt in high school, sopping wet and grinning on a trip to the Delaware Water Gap. It was the picture Julie had spent so many hours staring at back when she'd first come out to Madison and she and Matt had been apart. Past. Definitely the past. Julie almost didn't recognize her own smile in the photo. Had she really ever been that happy?

She sighed. This apartment where she and Matt had shared their dreams—and made Danielle—it was the past, too. She went over to one of the windows and looked out onto the town Green. A girl with an armload of books chased after a boy, down the brick walkway that cut toward campus.

Julie suddenly felt completely closed in. A prisoner. She'd barely left the apartment since Danielle had died, except to go out to the cemetery. She'd been stuck here with her own misery-soaked feelings and memories. She needed to get out. Really out. Away from here. Away from Madison. She had to forget all of it, forget this whole part of her life. To go back in time and start again—have it come out differently.

Go back. An image flashed through her head of her bedroom at home—in Philly. Her blue-and-white bedroom with the white four-poster bed and rolltop desk and framed copy of the first article she'd ever published in her high-school newspaper. A girl's room. Not a woman's room or a wife's room. Not a bedroom she shared with Matt. Not a place where there'd ever been thoughts of Danielle. Just a cozy room with her parents downstairs to take care of her.

Julie felt a wave of homesickness. Life had been so simple back in that room, in that house. When Mom cooked her breakfast and made sure she got to school on time. When *she* was the child. She suddenly had a pressing longing to see her parents and her brother, to just sit out in the yard under the cherry tree the way she used to do.

She stared out onto the Madison Green. Home. That's what she needed. To go home. To her real home. This apartment in Madison held nothing but painful memories—memories with Matt that were just too much of a reminder of what she'd lost. This wasn't her home anymore.

Twenty-one

❧

"You planning on keeping your jacket on all evening?" Bailey asked Marion, kissing the top of her head.

Sitting at the edge of Bailey's bed, Marion watched him go over to the stereo, choose a CD, and put it on. She took off her jacket and put it next to her neatly. The sounds of soft jazz filled the room. But rather than soothe her, the music made her feel nervous.

"So, um, where's Stewart tonight?" Stewart was Bailey's roommate, a transfer student from Boston University.

"Out," Bailey said. He dug a silver cigarette lighter out of the pocket of his jeans and lit the candle on his bureau. Then he switched off the light. The candle flame sent flickers of light and shadow dancing across the walls. "And he's not coming back anytime soon."

"Oh. Um, that's good," Marion said, not at all convinced of her own words. She wondered if Bailey had made some kind of deal with Stewart so that he'd stay away. Last time she'd been over, she and Bailey had been hot and heavy, stretched out right in the middle of the floor, when Stewart had come home and broken up the private party.

Actually, she'd been a little relieved. Sometimes she felt so out of control with Bailey, as if his kisses put her under his power, his spell. The sensible part of her seemed to fly right out the window. *Here I am, wolf. Bon appétit!* Bailey was so certain of himself, so much less tentative than Fred.

He came over and tossed her jacket on the floor. He sat down close to her and pulled her into his arms. Marion's nervousness turned into a little electric tingle. Softly, he traced the line of her jaw. She let her eyes close. He cupped her face, and she felt his mouth brush hers.

She reached up and wrapped her arms around his shoulders. She could feel his sinewy muscles through his T-shirt. She kissed him back—long and hard.

"Nice," he murmured. His hands worked the curves of her body as they kissed again.

And again. Marion found herself slipping down onto the bed, Bailey on top of her. He kissed her neck, reaching under her blouse.

Marion made a halfhearted attempt to shift away. Bailey was going too fast—but it felt so good. He ran his fingers up and down her bare back. She felt herself thrill to his touch.

He pulled her up to sitting again, then kissed her very gently. "Mmm," he whispered. He pulled back and looked into her eyes. "You look so beautiful tonight," he said as he undid the top button of her blouse.

Marion felt herself blush. "Thanks," she whispered.

Too fast, Marion thought, watching Bailey's fingers skillfully undo the rest of her buttons. She felt paralyzed, unable to stop him. She gave a little shiver. *What am I doing?*

Bailey tugged his own shirt over his head and tossed it away. He put his arms back around her. Their bodies were so warm against each other, soft and bare and warm. Bailey eased her back down on the bed.

The little voice in her head gave way to a ripple of pure pleasure. Bailey let his lips draw a line from the top of her head right down to her stomach. She heard herself let out a throaty sigh. He covered her with soft kisses.

She ran her hands down his bare back and

his arms. She kissed the sensitive place under his Adam's apple. His fingers found the button of her jeans. A current of dangerous excitement ran through her.

Then Bailey took her hand and placed it on the button of his own jeans. She felt a jolt of fear. *Slow down,* said the voice inside her.

She took her hands off him and rolled away from him. "Bailey . . ." she said.

Bailey flopped over onto his back.

"Look, Bailey, I just—I'm not ready, okay?"

Bailey blew out a breath. "Marion, we've been going out for almost a month."

Marion felt a tremor of embarrassment. "Yeah . . ."

"Well, kissing's very nice and everything, but . . ." He reached out to stroke her bare stomach.

Marion pulled away.

"Oh, come on, Marion. What's the matter? Doesn't it feel good?"

Marion shrugged. "Yeah. It's not that. . . ."

"Then what? Me?"

She shook her head.

Bailey rolled his eyes. "You know, we're not in junior high school anymore." There was a definite note of exasperation in his voice.

Marion felt any passion draining away. Fred had never pushed her further than she wanted to go. "If that's all you want from me . . ." she said quietly, her sentence trailing off.

Bailey propped himself up on one elbow. "Marion, it's not *all* I want. But we're not kids anymore." He shook his head. "At least I'm not. Sometimes I think you're still the same little 4-H girl you were back in Spotford."

Marion felt a flush of embarrassment. "And what was so wrong with her? At least she was a nice person." She thought about how she'd broken up with Fred, and she felt awful.

Bailey gave a tight laugh. "Maybe too nice."

"Maybe too nice for *you*," Marion said. She felt humiliated and angry and exposed. She hurriedly buttoned up her blouse, then noticed she'd done it all wrong.

Bailey lay on the bed, not moving a muscle. Part of Marion wished he'd draw her back to him, tell her how sorry he was, tell her he wanted to be with her, that she was worth waiting for. But he didn't even turn to look at her as she left.

She closed the door behind her. A tear of frustration worked its way to the corner of her eye. How dare Bailey push her further than she wanted to go? How could she have let herself fall for a guy who would do that?

It had come to this. Matt sat at the kitchen

table, staring blankly at the note Julie had left for him. He tried to reread the letter, but his eyes were glazed over, filled with hurt and anger.

A note. She'd walked out without even telling him face to face. This morning he'd actually felt that today might be the day when she'd start to turn things around. It had been a beautiful morning. Bright sunshine, crisp November air; it was Julie's favorite type of day. When she'd hugged and kissed him before he'd left the apartment, he'd felt a glimmer of hope that today Julie was going to pick herself up and start to walk again.

But now Matt realized that his own hopeful imagination had created that myth. No, this morning when they'd embraced, Julie wasn't saying, "Hi, I'm back." It was more like, "Goodbye. I can't deal with the pain anymore."

Matt grabbed the note. He wanted to rip it up, but he stopped himself. He rested his elbows on the table and let his head drop into his hands. He'd been dumped right back in the cold, dark, lonely place that he'd been working so hard to get out of. No Danielle, and now no Julie.

He remembered telling her to do something for herself today. Well, she had—and left him in the dust. How could she? How could she have wordlessly packed her bags and left? After all, weren't they married? For richer or poorer, in sickness and in health, till death do us part?

Till death do us part. A cold horror spread through him. Did that mean the death of a daughter? Had Matt and Julie's marriage been buried along with Danielle's tiny casket?

Just a little more than a year ago they'd vowed a lifetime of togetherness. A lifetime. Forever. There had been some awfully rough times since then, but their love had endured, and as a result of their dedication, their marriage had begun to blossom.

Until this. Danielle's death was maybe more than either of them could bear. And certainly more than they could bear alone. Alone. Matt glanced back down at the letter. *Trust me. I know it will be better for us both if we start again, without each other. The pain is too great to go on together. The memories hurt too much. I'm sorry.*

Was it because Julie blamed Matt for Danielle's death? She said she didn't, but then why did her eyes look so empty when he looked into them? Where was the love he always used to see? Didn't Julie understand that being together was the only way they could find the strength to start to live again? Didn't she remember the way they'd been there for each other after Mary Beth and Mark died? How could she have left?

Too much pain, pick up and split. If you turn your back on all the problems, they'll disappear. Matt painfully recalled the day, nearly ten years ago, when his mother had done just that—and never returned. And now it was happening all over again. He felt his misery boiling into anger. He grabbed Julie's note and crumpled it up into a little ball.

"Damn you, Julie!" he said to the empty room, throwing the paper onto the floor and collapsing into a chair.

Twenty-two

Julie lay on her four-poster bed, her head propped up on a pile of blue and white throw pillows. Funny—she hadn't ever thought about how little-girlish her old room was, with the flouncy lace trim on her pale blue canopy and matching bedspread, the gallery of stuffed animals that she'd grown up with perched on a shelf, the poster of Bent Fender's drummer, Roger Gold, on the back of the door. Roger still looked pretty cute behind his drum set, with his spiky black hair and dangly silver earring, but Julie barely ever listened to Bent Fender anymore.

In the closet and her chest of drawers were old clothes Julie had gone through the day before. She remembered when that pink Fair Isle sweater had been her favorite, and when those worn-out deck shoes had been brand-new, but they didn't even look like her style anymore. Maybe it was Dahlia's sophisticated influence. The clothes here in her room in her parents' house looked so old-fashioned.

Julie frowned. She wasn't the person she once was—she'd grown up, changed since the day she left for college. But she felt as if there was nothing in front of her, either. That her future had disappeared the moment she'd stepped too hard on the gas pedal in Dahlia's car.

She was consumed by a wave of loneliness. All her old friends were off at college. Dolores was studying theater at Northwestern. Tori was nearby, at Temple, but she was too busy to come home much. No one was going to drop by the way her friends did in Madison. Julie sighed. She hadn't appreciated the support enough—a visit from Marion, a phone call from Nick or any of a number of other friends. And Dahlia—Julie felt ashamed of her angry words the other day in the restaurant.

She reached for the collection of short stories on her night table. She opened to where she'd dog-eared one of the pages, but then put the book down again. She didn't feel like reading.

Back in high school, she would have picked

up the telephone and called Matt. He would have whisked her off on some hike in the woods or a ride on his motorcycle, or a good double feature at the movies with lots of buttery, popcorn-flavored kisses at intermission.

Julie's loneliness spiraled. Was she going to lose Matt and her friends and her life in Madison on top of what she'd already lost? She knew she'd been hard on Matt, but his pain only made her pain worse. One plus one equaled Danielle. She couldn't get away from that. Not even after a four-hundred-mile bus trip back to Philadelphia.

There was a soft knock on the door. "Julie?" her mother asked.

"Come in."

Her father followed right behind. They came into the middle of the room and stood there looking mildly uncomfortable. "Sweetie, we'd like to talk to you," her mother said.

Julie sat up. "Sure. I'm not doing anything."

"Julie, we know that you're suffering terribly," her father said.

"And we know how you feel," her mother added. "Lord knows we do, after losing a child of our own."

Julie nodded. She'd heard it all before.

"And we want you to know that we're here for you, no matter what," her father said.

Her parents exchanged a look that Julie couldn't quite read. They looked back at her, and her mother cleared her throat nervously. "But your father and I think that perhaps you're doing the wrong thing, leaving Madison—leaving Matt."

Julie felt a beat of surprise. Her parents had been so against her marriage. True, they'd warmed up to Matt recently, but she'd never imagined they'd be telling her to go back to him.

"Honey, school has always been so important to you," her mother said.

"And to us," her father put in sternly.

So that's what it was. Her education. Her future. The future that stretched bleakly in front of her. "You know, there are plenty of schools right here in Philadelphia," she said defensively.

"And what about right now?" her father asked. "This semester? Are you going to just throw it all away?"

Julie shrugged crossly. How could they talk to her about school at a time like this?

"What about your dreams, honey? My daughter, the journalist." Her mother laughed softly. "What about your job? You were so excited about it when we visited this summer."

Those warm, sticky August days seemed

240

like years ago to Julie. Her dreams? Her job? Her ambitions? She couldn't find the energy even to think about those things.

"And, Julie, most important, we both think that you and Matt need each other right now," her mother said. "You know, when he was sick, we were so impressed by the way you took care of each other, the way you loved each other."

"Your sense of responsibility to each other," her father put in.

"And after the accident, when you were unconscious, Matt practically didn't leave the side of your bed," her mother said. "He was there for you, even though you didn't know it."

Julie felt a shiver of guilt. "And you think I'm not there for him," she said, her voice coming out defensively.

Her mother walked over to the bed and sat down next to her. "Honey, what we think is that you're hurting. More than you've ever hurt in your life. And that it can be hard to think clearly when your emotions are so strong." She put a gentle hand on Julie's shoulder.

Julie pulled away. "Are you saying that you want me to leave?"

"No. No, of course not, sweetheart. You're welcome here as long as you want. We've— well, we haven't been as close over the last few years as we once were, and we're glad we can be together again. We want to be close again, Julie."

Julie felt a rawness in her throat. She blinked back a tear. "I want to be close again, too," she said softly. Why was she getting angry with her mother and father? They were just trying to help her.

"But not this way. We don't want to have you here because you're hiding your head in the sand," her father said.

"So don't keep hiding from your life," her mother said.

Julie felt the tears begin to spill. "I'm not hiding," she said. "I just . . ." Just what? Couldn't face her life? Couldn't face Madison? Or Matt? Maybe she *was* hiding.

"Julie," her mother said. "We hope you're thinking about going back home."

Home? Where was home? Julie wondered. No, it wasn't here anymore. But she didn't feel much like it was in Madison, either.

"I think this is yours," Nick said frostily.

Dahlia had barely peeled her eyes open, and she was still snuggled under the covers. She wouldn't even have been awake yet, except that Nick had been up cleaning the room and making sure that he let her know about it. She'd been pried from some warm dream by banging drawers, rustling papers, and loud footsteps.

Now, what had she been dreaming about? Dahlia couldn't pull it to the surface. *I was probably being taken on a whirlwind tour of Rome by some handsome Italian guy,* she thought sourly. Nick was still standing frozen by his desk, holding up a pen—or was it a pencil?

"The teeth marks," he stated. "The chewed-up pencils are yours." He tossed the pencil onto Dahlia's desk. There was a pile of papers and books he'd dumped there, too, and a mountain of her clothing that he'd heaped on her desk chair, so that it could get totally wrinkled.

Dahlia rolled her eyes. *Here I am with some mysterious Roman boyfriend, and Nick has to wake me up so I can watch him move pencils from his desk to mine.*

"Fine, Nick. I won't dare make the mistake of leaving a pencil on your desk again," she said, her voice still heavy with sleep. "I mean, anything of mine might have cooties. By the way, good morning."

Nick flashed her a frown. "Look, there are two of us who have to live in this room, you know. Unfortunately," he added. Dahlia felt a prickle of hurt. "And you think you can just trash the place. I know you had a maid at home to pick up all your stuff . . ." he went on.

Dahlia's hurt turned to anger. "Oh, the little

243

rich-girl number again. Nick, spare me."

"No, you spare me. I don't want to be cleaning up after you all the time."

"So don't. The mess never seemed to bother you before."

"Maybe I just didn't say anything."

Dahlia sat up. "Listen, I have an idea. Why don't you just stretch a piece of masking tape down the middle of the floor? This side's yours and this side's mine. Don't put a foot over this line." She gave a nervous laugh. "Let Mother and Daddy check that out if they think there's anything improper going on here."

Nick ignored her remark. Dahlia studied the set of his handsome face, the tension in his shoulders under his blue work shirt. It was as if he wanted to be angry with her. And this little rich-girl stuff—it was really something from their past. She thought he knew her better by now. But she was obviously wrong.

She watched him stomp around the room some more, hanging up his own clothes and making twice as much noise as he had to. *Do I really need this?* Dahlia thought. Nick was making her feel as if she was the most awful person in the world. Why? Because she had a wonderful, exciting opportunity next semester, and she was actually thinking about taking it.

She wondered why she was even hedging.

What was the point of even considering staying in Madison now? So that Nick could freeze her out of her own room? So that she could destroy Paul and Maya's happy little love nest? So that her parents could find out what was going on and raise the roof—even though she and Nick weren't even talking, let alone doing anything her mother and father could disapprove of? Why stay here? So that she could be as miserable as she'd been feeling for the past few weeks?

And with Julie back in Philadelphia, there wasn't even any reason to stick around for her. Julie had needed to pick up and leave, and she'd done it. *Why can't I do the same?* Dahlia thought.

"Nick," she said. She took a deep breath.

He stopped where he was, in the middle of the room. "Yeah?" he asked guardedly.

"I've decided that I'm going to Italy next semester." The words fell with a kind of finality. Dahlia felt a mixture of relief and sadness and total panic. She'd essentially just kissed Nick good-bye. Well, not exactly kissed. They didn't do that anymore. That was the problem. So, on to new things, new adventures—new people.

Nick's face was expressionless. He gave a curt nod. "Fine," he said flatly. "I hope you have a wonderful time."

245

Twenty-three

๛

He'd been riding for nearly an hour. Fast, into a frigid November wind, along the highway outside Madison. Just to escape. To escape from his own fear and anger. Too much blame and too much guilt. He needed to stop tormenting himself. Sitting all day in the apartment waiting to hear from Julie had only made it worse. So many times in the past two days, he'd been about to pick up the phone and call her. But each time, his anger stopped him. Julie had left *him*. Let her be the one to get in touch. Let her call.

When he'd reached his boiling point, he'd bundled up and hopped on his motorcycle. No particular destination in mind, he'd just needed to get out, to find a way to forget about Julie and Danielle, if only for a brief while.

But even on the wide-open road, at seventy-five miles an hour, Matt couldn't shake the pain. It was just as lonely outside in the ice-cold darkness as it was back in the apartment.

Company, not solitude, was what he really needed. He thought of going to visit Nick, but he knew that would mean a heavy-duty talk about Julie's leaving. Leon would respond by playing the blues, which Matt had had enough of today. What he needed was a big, boisterous crowd. He needed to party it off. Noise, people, action.

The next thing he knew, he was pushing open the front door to the Barn and Grill. He'd never been the type to hang out at work on his night off, but going back home and waiting for a call that wasn't going to come was out of the question. At least there were people here. People out to have fun.

"A little early for Thursday lunch," Jake called out to him from behind the bar. "You leave something here?"

Matt unzipped his leather jacket, forced a smile, and walked up to the bar. "Nah. I just needed to get out of the house for a while." He spotted an empty stool and sat down. "How's it going, Jake?"

"Haven't you had enough of us, buddy?" Jake asked, scraping some of the foam off the top of a pitcher of beer and placing it back under the tap to fill it until it overflowed. "Hey, Bailey, another one for Carl's table."

"Yeah, Bailey," Carl chortled. "You heard the boss man. We're almost empty over here."

"Chill!" Bailey hollered back from the kitchen window, where he was getting an order of burgers and fries from Pat.

"You rode all the way out in the cold for another night of this?" Jake laughed.

Matt shrugged. "It's sort of nice being here and not having to deal with any of the trouble," he said, rolling his eyes in Carl's direction.

"Yeah, sure. I suppose." Jake gave him a long look. "You okay, Matt?"

"Yeah, sure," Matt said flatly. He looked around the room. Marcy and her pals were at their usual table, a couple of baskets of fries and glasses of beer in front of them. Carl's gang was drinking up a storm in the corner. On the college side, two huge groups of Madison students were munching on burgers. Another table of college kids sat with an older man who must be their professor. He was talking, and they were scribbling notes as he spoke.

A typical night at the Barn and Grill, with everything and everyone in its proper place. Everyone except Matt and Julie. He had a sudden picture of Julie, back in Philadelphia with her family. It didn't make sense.

"Hey, Matt, what's shakin'?" Bailey came up from behind and grabbed the pitcher from the counter.

"How's it going, Bailey? Raking in the tips tonight?"

"Hardly. I should have scored big, though. Some creep with a bankroll came in earlier and dropped a wad on champagne. Made a big impression on his girl, but he stiffed me cold in the end."

"Welcome to the Barn and Grill."

"Yeah, well, one day I'll get even with the jerk." He started to walk away with the pitcher and then turned back toward Matt. "What are you doing here on your night off, anyway, man? Julie didn't come with you? Did you guys duke it out or something?"

"Yo, Bailey. I think Carl's thirsty," Jake said, bringing the conversation to a halt. "That kid never seems to stop," he said when Bailey was out of earshot.

"He's okay," Matt said.

"Yeah, I suppose." Jake exhaled a hefty breath of air. "But he's got to learn a little subtlety. I mean the kid—"

"Hey, Jake, it's all right," Matt insisted. "It's just his way of being friendly. Besides, I can take care of myself. You don't have to protect me."

Matt felt Jake's scrutinizing eyes on him. "You *sure* you're okay, Matt?" he asked.

Matt nodded.

"How about Julie? She feeling a little better?"

Matt shrugged. "I suppose. You know, *I* might feel a little better if you'd offer me something to drink. I'm a customer now, remember? How about pouring me a beer?"

"Sure, when you're twenty-one."

"Come on, Jake." Matt shrugged. "It's just a beer."

"I suppose you're going to pull out a fake ID next."

"Is that what a guy needs around here to get himself a beer?"

"Since when are you drinking, anyway? I thought you had your last one a long time ago."

Matt looked away.

"What's wrong, Matt?"

Matt tried to ignore the concern in Jake's voice. "I just felt like having a beer, that's all," Matt snapped. "Jeez, Jake, just this once. What's the big deal?"

But Jake wasn't budging. "You're starting to sound like the pimply high-school kids who beg me to serve them every Friday and Saturday." He reached for a glass, placed it under the soft-drink dispenser, and filled it with orange soda.

"On the house," he said as he put it in front of Matt. "How about a burger or something to go with it?"

"You know what I want." Just a beer. One lousy beer. He wasn't going to line up the bar with empty glasses. Just have a drink or two to take the edge off the hurt. After everything that had happened, who could really blame him? "This is a joke, right? Back in Philly they served me when I was sixteen. No big deal. If I needed to unwind, I'd have a drink. Or two or three. And nobody told me I couldn't."

But as he heard the words coming out of his mouth, Matt knew right away how strange they sounded. It was as if somebody else were inside doing the talking.

Back when he was sixteen, he had been fearless. Nothing stopped him or his friends from testing the limits. Not until Mary Beth and Mark went over the line, and paid for it with their lives. That was the night that being fearless lost its meaning. It was the night the drinking stopped, too.

"Jake, I'm sorry. Really I am. I don't know what came over me. I—I've had a pretty lousy day."

Jake turned toward Matt. His warm smile seemed to say that he understood. "What about that burger?"

Matt nodded. "Sure, okay."

"Bailey, bring Matt a burger, huh? Rare, melted Swiss, lettuce, tomato, and grilled onions. Right?" he asked.

"You got it." Matt smiled.

By the time the burger came, Matt had told Jake everything about Julie going home. He'd come to the Barn and Grill to forget about it all, but in the end, he couldn't pass up the sympathetic ear of a good friend. Jake had always been someone whose opinion Matt valued.

"Now I'm the one who wants the beer," Jake admitted after hearing the story.

Matt laughed. "Try the orange soda. It's real potent."

"Any ideas?" Jake asked. "I mean, what now?"

"I could call her," Matt said. "Except I'm too mad. Besides, if the past few weeks are anything to go by, she'll just clam right up—not say a word. Doesn't seem to be much use in holding my ear to a silent phone receiver," he said morosely.

"Then you're going to wait," Jake said. "Until she decides to come home."

"*If* she decides to come home." Matt picked up his burger and started to take a bite. But he had no appetite. Not even for Pat's famous burger. Madison without Julie. It didn't make sense. She was the reason he'd come here. To be with his best friend. To bask in her smile. To feel the warmth of her body. He thought about the softness of her lips on his face, her scent. "You know, as angry as I am, I'd just like to put my arms around her and hug her," Matt admitted.

Jake arched an eyebrow. "Well, now we're getting somewhere."

"We are?"

Jake nodded. "If you want to hug her, why don't you go do it? I think your bosses could arrange a few days off."

"You mean go to Philly?"

"Go and talk to her. Hug her. Show her how much you love her."

It sounded good in theory, but Matt felt an ache of despair. Julie had run away. Julie had turned her back on him. Why would it be any different in Philadelphia? An all-night ride on his motorcycle so he could get turned away?

An all-night ride. A ride to Julie. Matt gave a bitter laugh. "You know, this reminds me a little bit of the way it was before I came out to Madison. Man, it seems like a million years ago. Julie and I had this terrible fight on the phone. We felt so far away from each other. I just couldn't stand it a second longer, so I jumped on my bike and rode all night until I got out here."

Jake began laughing. Matt arched an eyebrow. "You want to let me in on the joke?"

"Well, that turned out pretty well, as I understand the story. Seems like it could work again."

Matt felt a glimmer of hope. But it was quickly doused. "Jake, after that last ride, Julie and I made some very serious vows. For better or for worse. I don't think that means bailing out and going home to Mom and Dad."

"Then you're going to hang around Madison and come drown your sorrows in orange soda every night?" Jake asked. He didn't wait for an answer. He pushed the plate with the burger on it toward Matt. "Eat up, man. You've got a long trip ahead of you."

Twenty-four

❧

"Honey," Julie's mother called from the other room. "There's someone here to see you."

Julie got up and turned off the television in the den. She hadn't really been following the program she'd turned on—something about releasing bald eagles born in captivity into the wild—but she hadn't heard the doorbell, either. She felt a flutter of curiosity. A visitor? For her?

Probably just one of her parents' friends, full of concern and good intentions. She knew she should appreciate the effort, but she hoped it wasn't one of the ladies from her father's church, like the one who'd stopped by yesterday and smiled sadly at her with such big, puppy-dog eyes. Julie didn't want to be reminded of what an awful blow she'd been dealt. She didn't want to have to be polite and say she was going to be fine. She wasn't fine.

Maybe if someone would just tell her a good joke, she thought, leaving the den and stepping out into the hall. She heard voices in the foyer, near the front door.

"I'm so glad to see you," her mother was saying. "You must be freezing cold. Can I fix you something to eat or drink?"

Despite herself, Julie's curiosity quickened her step. She let out a little gasp. Matt was standing by the door in his jeans and leather jacket, his motorcycle helmet in his hands. She found herself instantly happy to see him—but her happiness was tempered by a funny kind of shame, as if she'd been caught doing something she shouldn't have been doing. In this case, leaving Matt wounded and alone, without even a word in person.

"Matt," she said, feeling herself blush.

"Julie." He took a step toward her, as if he were going to wrap his arms around her, but then he seemed to reconsider. He shifted awkwardly from one boot to the other.

"Um, do you want to come sit down?" Julie asked, feeling rather silly. Especially in front of her mother. Here was her husband and she had to invite him inside, as if he was a formal visitor.

"Matt!" came a loud, whooping voice from

upstairs, followed by Julie's brother Tommy flying down the staircase.

"Sport!" Matt didn't stop himself from folding Tommy into a big bear hug. Julie felt a ripple of envy. And a touch of relief. After the accident, Tommy had been angry at Matt—as if he had needed someone to blame, a guilty party to make sense of a senseless tragedy. Now Tommy seemed ready to put that behind him. Julie knew she could learn a lesson from her little brother.

"Wow, Matt, you're really here," Tommy said.

"I am, and it's great to see you," Matt said. "But listen, sport, I need a little time with your sister, okay? Then we'll hang out."

"Yeah, I know," Tommy said reasonably. Julie felt a pinch of sadness. This was all so difficult for her brother, too. Not too long ago, he would have grumbled and pouted and insisted that Matt come right up to his room to check out his new dirt-bike magazine or his new in-line skates.

"Tommy, why don't you come help me in the kitchen?" Julie's mother said. "Matt's had a long, cold trip. I'm sure he could use something to warm him up."

"Thanks, Mrs. Miller. I could," Matt agreed. They headed toward the kitchen, and Julie and Matt were alone.

"So, um, should we go sit in the living room?" Julie asked uncomfortably.

"Usual spot on the green sofa," Matt said with deliberate lightness.

Julie managed a little laugh. "Our old spot." She noticed Matt's face was pink from cold. "How was your ride? It's really winter out today. You must be frozen after riding here all the way from Madison."

Matt shrugged. "I hardly noticed. I was too busy thinking about you."

Julie led the way into the living room. "I'm sorry," she said softly. Matt tossed his helmet on the armchair and took off his gloves and jacket. They settled down on the sofa.

"Don't be." Matt took one of her hands.

"Ahh!" His hands were freezing. Julie took them both in hers and began to rub them.

Matt smiled. "Mmm. Worth the whole trip," he said. "I missed you."

"I missed you, too," Julie said. It was the truth. She'd been so lonely the couple of days she'd been home. She'd had plenty of long hours to remember all the good times she and Matt had together during their last two years of high school—and the wonderful times they'd shared since they'd been married. Several times she'd almost picked up the telephone to call him, but then the pain of Danielle's death would sweep over her and she'd find herself paralyzed.

Matt leaned toward her and kissed her cheek. Julie could feel his hesitation. She turned her face toward his and kissed him back, on the lips, encouragingly. He responded, softly but lingeringly. She could feel some of his hesitation disappearing. His kisses were familiar, comforting—and at the same time, Julie felt a tingle of excitement.

She wrapped her arms around him. "Mmm. It really is good to have you here, Matt." She kissed his dark eyebrows and the closed lids of his eyes, running her fingers through his thick, dark hair.

He stroked the side of her face, gently, tenderly. She could feel the love in his caress. She found her lips seeking his again. She and Matt hadn't kissed this way since before Danielle had died. Julie felt the loneliness of her days in Philadelphia melting away. This felt good. This felt right.

Their bodies pressed together, straining to be even closer. Julie ran her hands up Matt's back, under his sweater. They didn't stop kissing as they slipped down on the sofa.

Suddenly Matt bolted upright. Julie sat up, too. "What?" she asked.

Matt's gaze darted around the room. He had

a guilty look on his face. "Your folks," he said. "Your mom's going to come in here any second with a hot chocolate, or something. And here we are . . ."

"Kissing," Julie supplied. She felt a bubble of laughter forming inside her. "Yeah, we're stealing a few kisses. Matt, we *are* married, you know. I think it's allowed."

Matt laughed, too. "Oh. Yeah, hey. I guess I'm so used to sitting right in this spot and having that 'door open, one foot on the floor' rule your father made for us. Well, guess what, Reverend Miller? Your daughter is my wife!" He pulled Julie toward him and gave her an overdone, television kiss.

He and Julie cracked up. Julie felt a world of tension dissolving in her laughter. The laughter started deep in her belly and flooded through her whole body. It felt so incredible. She'd thought she might never be able to laugh like this again. She abandoned herself to the feeling, gulping in huge breaths of air.

And then, without warning, her laughter turned suddenly to tears. "Oh, Matt," she sobbed.

"Hey, hey," he said softly. "Are you crying?" He drew her close and stroked her hair. "Go ahead. That's right."

The crying felt as good as the laughter, in its

own way. Julie sobbed in Matt's arms. As her crying began to quiet down, he took her face in his hands and kissed her wet cheeks.

"Julie, I love you," he whispered.

"I love you, too." As she said it, she knew it was true, in spite of the despair of losing Danielle. "Matt, I'm so sorry. I'm sorry I've hurt you. I missed you. I've been so lonely."

"Me, too," Matt said. "It felt so awful to have the person I love most in the whole world run away from me."

Julie bit her lip. "Not from you, Matt. From how much it hurt. The memories, the pain. Walking past Elm Street and thinking, *the road to the hospital.* Or else it was the road to the cemetery. The place where the accident happened. Whatever. That's what I was running away from."

"And maybe running just a little from me— the one who was too stubborn to trade my bike in for a car? One that worked right?" Matt's voice was filled with the agony of guilt.

A silence stretched between them. Julie shifted uncomfortably on the sofa. "Well, maybe I *was* angry. Maybe I am, and I didn't really want to admit it. At you, at Dahlia. But mostly at myself. Matt, you weren't the one driving that car."

"Julie, it was an accident," Matt said. "Accident, as in no one's fault."

Julie shook her head. "Tell that to yourself."

"I'm trying. You know how hard it is. Like somehow, if you're responsible, you should be able to make it come out differently."

Julie laughed sadly. "I know exactly what you mean. I keep replaying that moment and I'm going slower, more in control . . ."

Matt stroked the side of her face. "Jules, no one can make it come out differently. Not me or you or Dahlia or anyone. She's gone." His voice cracked, and Julie saw tears forming in the corners of his deep-set eyes.

She felt a fresh onslaught of her own tears. The tears she'd been holding in, the tears she'd been too empty to cry. She and Matt held each other, sharing the sobs that shook their bodies. Julie held on to him as if an anchor in a wild, stormy sea.

"I'm glad you're here," she said, her tears subsiding at last. "I'm glad you came."

"Come home," Matt said. "Please, Julie."

Julie wiped her eyes with the back of her hand. She didn't say anything.

"At least think about it," Matt begged. "Julie, you have a life in Madison. School, a job, friends who love you. And me. You have me, and I'm there. I'm still there. Well, I mean, I'm here right now, but I live there."

Julie laughed softly. "I know what you mean."

"Then you'll give it another try?"

She shrugged. A picture of Danielle's tiny grave came into her mind, and she felt a shiver of fear. How could she go back to the place that reminded her of the worst tragedy of her life?

"Julie, don't you want to be the kind of person who Danielle would have wanted her mother to be?" Matt asked gently.

The person who Danielle would have wanted me to be . . . Why, she'd never asked herself what would have made Danielle proud. Never thought about it that way. Certainly running away to her parents' house in Philadelphia wasn't anything to be proud of. Leaving all her responsibilities—and her friends. She thought about what her mother and father had reminded her of the other day—that every day she spent away from school was one day that took her further away from graduation. Did she really want to be a college dropout? She hadn't planned it that way. She hadn't planned anything. She'd just run from the pain.

But how could she possibly face it again? How could she visit Danielle's tiny headstone, and then just forget about it and turn back to her books? How could she sit in their living room on Main Street in the exact place where Danielle was supposed to have slept? How could she make a future when everything reminded her of a gruesome past?

"I don't know, Matt." She shook her head over and over. "I just don't know."

Twenty-five

Marion sipped her ginger ale slowly. *You don't want to call him,* she told herself. The guy was just out to get what he could; he didn't care about her. He was a—well, wolf. The problem was that he was an awfully sexy wolf.

She glanced around the campus snack bar. Several groups of kids were hanging out, laughing and talking, and a number of couples shared fries, sodas, and gooey gazes. At an orange vinyl corner booth a lanky, long-faced girl Marion often saw at the library had her nose in a thick book and was taking copious notes.

Marion slurped her soda. Maybe Bailey would just happen to walk by. He'd see her sitting here, and come over, and give her one of those kisses. . . .

Forget it, she told herself. He wanted something she didn't want to give him, and he was going to push until he got it. She'd found that out the other night. Maybe she'd even known it all along, but hadn't wanted to admit it. Maybe she and Bailey could be friends one day, but the wolf and the 4-H girl just didn't belong together as a couple. Then why was it she couldn't get the guy off her mind? She felt a sizzle of frustration.

She watched as the door from Central Bowl was pushed open, half hoping to see Bailey's dark head of hair, his well-built body, half hoping not to. Instead, she felt a jolt of surprise as Fred's carrot-colored mop appeared. She felt herself freeze, ginger ale in hand. Fred glanced around the snack bar. Their eyes met.

Marion raised her hand in a stiff little wave. Fred waved back and smiled. His funny, eager smile. Marion realized she'd missed it. She was glad that Fred didn't seem angry at her anymore. Maybe enough time had passed since that evening she and Bailey had run into him on the street. She hoped Fred missed her, too. He made his way over to her table.

"Hi," he said.

"Hi, Fred." Marion felt a combination of eagerness and shyness.

"Doing your physics?" he asked. The text

was open in front of her, but she hadn't been reading it.

She shrugged. "Trying to. It's pretty complicated. And noisy in here," she added.

Fred peered at the book, and she could see him trying to read it upside down. "Oh, the spin of elementary particles. Cool stuff. You know, all they really mean is what a particle looks like from different directions. The famous physicist Stephen Hawking says it helps if you think of the particles as a deck of cards—some of them look the same turned upside down as right side up. Like the seven of diamonds, for instance. Some of them look different. Ace of clubs."

Marion nodded slowly. "Oh. Now it's starting to make sense. That's kind of neat. Listen, you want to sit down?" She nodded at the chair across from her.

Fred tugged nervously at the brim of his baseball cap. "I—um—I'd like that, but, ah—well, what I'm trying to say is that I'm meeting someone here." The end of his sentence came out in a jumbled rush.

"Oh." Someone. A girl someone? Marion got a funny feeling in her stomach. Wasn't Fred still pining away over her?

Fred glanced around the snack bar. "Here she is now." Marion followed his gaze. A short, sweet-faced girl with blond, shoulder-length hair was coming toward them.

"Hi, Fred," she said shyly. She cast an inquisitive glance at Marion.

"Uh, Jan, this is Marion. Marion, Jan."

Marion rose slightly from her chair and extended her hand. "Pleased to meet you," she said, not at all sure it was true.

"Same," Jan said.

There was a moment of awkward silence. "Well," Fred said, "I guess we'll be seeing you, Marion."

"Okay, see you," Marion echoed. She watched Fred and Jan head for an empty corner booth.

I guess we'll be seeing you. We. Fred had managed to find somebody new awfully quickly. She felt a tickle of jealousy. What had she thought? That Fred would wait around for her forever, in case she changed her mind? Had she changed her mind? Marion sighed. She didn't think so.

So what did she want?

Waiting for Julie again. Waiting in his old bedroom in Philly. It was a pale November afternoon. The sun was barely visible through a thick blanket of gray clouds. The swaying oaks outside the window were shedding their final few brown leaves.

Matt had reached for the phone at least a half-dozen times, but he had never actually dialed Julie's number. He'd already said everything he could when he'd seen her the night before. At first he'd thought his words had gotten through. He'd thought that she was ready to try to leave the guilty feelings behind, that she was ready to embrace her life again—the pain and the joy. He'd thought that when they'd held each other, it meant she was ready to come home.

But here he was—still waiting. Lying on his old bed, in his old room, in a place that was no longer his home. He looked around at the rock-and-roll posters that covered his walls, at the stacks of sports and motorcycle magazines on his shelves—mementos of the years he had lived here. It was strange. A year ago, when he'd first gotten out to Madison, all he could think and dream about was coming home. Back to Philly, back to the good friends and good times. He glanced at a photo of him and his friend Steven hiking in the Poconos. What a day that was, just the two of them challenging the snow-capped peaks in midwinter. There was a another photo of Matt deejaying a party at his father's club—another favorite memory.

But that's what they were, memories. Fresh in his mind, maybe, but they'd happened a lifetime ago. So much had changed since then. He couldn't just step back into the past. Madison was his home now. He'd gotten married the day after he'd gotten there. He'd launched a career that was now on the verge of taking off. He'd battled and defeated cancer there. Nick and Leon and his other friends were there. Matt wanted to be there, too. But he wanted to be there with Julie.

On top of the dresser was a photo of the two of them. Framed in silver, they were hugging each other, both of them in their green-and-gold high-school graduation gowns. Matt remembered the two of them that day, tossing their caps high in the air and then wrapping their arms around each other. He remembered that moment well because he had made a silent wish that he and Julie would stay together forever. And looking into her eyes after they'd hugged, he was sure Julie had made the same wish.

Hadn't she? Hadn't she meant it in the passionate letters she'd sent him from Madison last fall when he was still back in Philly? Her letters, like her eyes when she'd looked at him on their wedding day, were filled with promise and hope for a future together. When she'd vowed *I do* in Riverville last year, Matt had believed it. If only Julie would remember Riverville, really remember how deeply they'd meant what they'd said . . .

Matt thought about getting out of the house for a little while and trying to relax. Steven was probably back from classes by now. They could go for a ride, or just hang out. Or maybe his dad could use some help at the Fast Lane, setting up for tonight's band. That might help temporarily. But it wasn't going to provide any real solution if he turned to the past to help with the future. No, it wouldn't work.

The only sensible thing to do was to go back to Madison—to his job, his apartment, his friends. With or without Julie, it was time to go home. He'd make his bed, leave a note for his dad, and be off. If he rode fast, he could get out there in time to help Pat and Jake close up tonight.

Then why, he wondered, if he was in such a rush to get back, was it taking so long to make his bed and write a note? He labored over folding and refolding his blankets. He struggled to write a short note to his dad, crumpling it up and starting again at least five times. *Dad, thanks for everything.* He couldn't just leave a few words on a piece of paper for his father to find when he got home. Maybe he should wait, say good-bye to his dad in person. He paced his room, glancing out the window into the front yard.

His spirits soared toward the roof. Julie was coming up the brick walkway, carrying a bulging backpack. *For her return trip to Madison?* Matt barreled down the stairs and raced to the front door. He pulled it open. He wanted to scoop Julie up in his arms and pull her close. But what if he was wrong about why she was here?

Julie stood on the front step, her eyes unable to meet Matt's. She wrapped a nervous finger around a lock of brown hair. "I—I thought you might have left already."

"I was about to."

"I'm glad you're still here."

"There's a chance, then?" Matt asked.

Julie paused, then nodded.

"You're with me?" He held out his hand.

She hesitated at first, then put her hand out for him to take. "I've always been with you. As hard as I tried to run away from everything, I couldn't." She looked up. Her big brown eyes were moist.

"Julie." Matt drew her close and she fell into his hold, trembling, clutching onto him with all her strength.

"I love you, Matt." Her tears began to flow. "I can't run away anymore. Not from you, and not from Danielle. I do want to be someone she would have been proud of."

They held on to each other for a long time. Julie's tears brought on a burst of Matt's own, a salty mixture of sorrow and joy.

In the open doorway, the fresh air felt rejuvenating. When their lips touched, Matt felt his whole body flooded with joy. *For richer, for poorer, for better, for worse, through sickness and in health, for all the days of our lives, until death do us part . . .*

Twenty-six

Marion picked up a gray-red, fist-size stone from the cold, hard ground at the edge of the quarry. She held it in her upturned palm and gently bounced her hand up and down, feeling the stone's weight. Then she closed her fingers around it, drew her arm back, and hurled the stone as far as she could into the middle of the quarry. It made a satisfying plunk as it broke the water's surface. Marion watched as ripples of water spread out in concentric circles around where the rock had sunk. She found another rock and threw it, too. Threw away her anger at Bailey. Threw away her sadness about Fred.

When she'd first come to Madison, she'd thought having a boyfriend would be the be-all and end-all. She remembered thinking how incredibly lucky Julie was to have Matt. The tears

Julie shed reading Matt's letters at the beginning of last year only proved how special their love was.

And Dahlia. Back at that first picnic outside the dorm, Marion could just tell that Dahlia had had all kinds of boyfriends—and that she could just snap her fingers and there'd be a dozen more guys lining up for her.

Marion found an especially large stone and threw it into the water. Back when she was a freshman, she'd thought that if only she had a boyfriend, she'd be the happiest person on campus. And then she'd met Fred. She gave a bittersweet laugh, thinking about how long it had taken to get Fred to kiss her. Once he'd gotten started, though, there was no stopping him. That first time, he and Marion had wound up so lost in each other that they'd gotten locked into the Madison Museum's outdoor sculpture garden after hours and had practically had to turn cartwheels all night to keep from freezing. That night she'd found out that kissing had done the trick even better than gymnastics.

Despite the numb fingers and toes and the chattering teeth, Marion had been filled with warmth and electric excitement. She couldn't get enough of Fred's nearness. And then it had worn off. What had happened? Was it all the time they'd spent together? Did the specialness of someone's kisses simply fade away after a while? Or had she really outgrown Fred, changed when he hadn't?

Marion had been so sure she needed someone new, someone different, more exciting. Enter Bailey. But she'd gone from wrong to more wrong. So who *was* right for her? What was she looking for? she asked herself. She felt a ripple of confusion spreading out around her, like the ripples on the water around the stones.

Maybe she needed to figure out some answers for herself before she started looking around for Mr. Right. Whoever he was. How long had it been since she'd just spent some time by herself this way? She thought about how she used to do it all the time on the farm— take a walk in the cornfields or lie in the haystack in the barn. No homework, no music on her Walkman, just the sounds of nature and her own thoughts.

She threw another rock. The ripples spread out from the center in wave after wave. *Like light waves emanating from a distant star,* Marion thought. Or the pulses given off by the subatomic particles that made up everything on the planet.

Standing by the edge of the quarry, the clouds low, a lone winter bird chirping, Marion felt suddenly awed by the world around her. And the world inside her and above her. Maybe she'd be an astrophysicist one day, studying far-away galaxies, she thought. Although after her human biology class last year, she'd been sure she was going to be a physician.

Marion smiled. That was really why she was here at Madison. Sure, the boys were part of it. And so were all the friends she'd made. Julie, Gwen, Susan—even Dahlia was becoming a pal. But the main reason she'd come to school was to learn all the things she wanted to know—and to learn about herself.

Yeah, that was the answer. She needed to find out who she was, who she wanted to be. Maybe that had to come first in order to know who she wanted to be with.

Dahlia and Nick sat in the middle of Julie and Matt's apartment, surrounded by several plastic trash bags full of tiny clothes, toys, and stuffed animals.

"Thanks for helping me," Nick said stiffly. He took a pink plastic rattle out of one of the bags and packed it into a cardboard box filled with other baby things. "I really don't know if I could deal by myself."

Dahlia picked up a tiny pair of softly faded overalls—a present from her to Danielle. "I know what you mean." For a moment she pictured the baby she'd visited in the hospital, but grown chubby and healthy enough to fit into the overalls, smiling and bouncing on Julie's lap. She felt a stab of pain, and banished the image. It hurt too much to think about what might have been.

"When Matt and I took the baby furniture down to the basement, we just dumped all this stuff in these bags. Matt couldn't stand to look at it for a second more than he had to."

"I can understand," Dahlia said. She folded the overalls and packed them away with the rest of the clothes. She sneaked a glance at Nick. His green eyes were moist. "You know, it was really nice of you to think about getting the apartment ready before those guys get home."

Nick looked up at her, surprise flashing across his fine-featured face. "Me? Nice?" he said. His voice was a funny mixture of bitterness and sadness.

Dahlia felt herself growing defensive. "Hey, give me a break, Nick. I'm just saying that you're a good friend to those guys. Just take the compliment, okay?"

Nick gave a clipped laugh. "Well, okay. I guess I'm just not used to getting compliments from you these days."

"Likewise," Dahlia said. She packed away a tiny purple-and-yellow striped hat. She thought she remembered Julie saying it was a present from Maya. L.A. Lakers' colors. Maya was a loyal fan of her hometown basketball team.

Nick let out a noisy breath. "Look, Dahlia, I'm sorry things have been so bad between us."

Dahlia bit her lip. Now he got around to that? After he'd turned their room into the Cold War revisited? After she'd already decided that she was leaving next semester? Nick's apology was too late.

"Did you ever think about how we started fighting right around the time of Julie's accident?" Nick continued. "And it got worse after Danielle died." He closed one of the boxes and taped the flaps shut with duct tape. "Maybe the sadness was too much, you know? It's been hard on all of us."

Dahlia couldn't disagree. She stored away a tiny pair of tie-dyed socks and a matching T-shirt. "Look, I'm sure it didn't make me the nicest person in the world, watching my best friend fall apart." She took a breath. "And knowing it was my own fault."

Nick shook his head. "Why? Because you lent Julie your car? You think being generous with your friends is a fault? Dahlia, you didn't realize there was a problem."

"I should have."

Nick frowned. "Yeah, well I should have, too. You might remember that we drove halfway across the country together in that car. And that I did plenty of the driving. I'd heard the brakes, too. You think it's my fault?"

Dahlia felt a current of surprise. Through all the bad weeks with Nick, through all her anger, it had never once occurred to her to split the blame with him. How could Nick know that a metallic squeal of brakes forecast death? And if Nick couldn't know, why did she hold herself responsible?

"Let go of it, Dahlia," Nick said softly. "Julie and Matt need our friendship, not someone to blame."

Dahlia shrugged. "Julie must hate me."

"You don't really believe that, do you?" Nick asked. "Julie doesn't hate you." There was a moment's pause. "I don't hate you," he said, almost like an echo. Dahlia felt herself drawn to his gaze. There was a funny little flutter in her stomach. "I've missed you," he said.

"You have?"

"Yeah."

Dahlia felt herself leaning toward Nick. Closer. Suddenly, she pulled back. "What about my trip?" The fluttery feeling vanished. "Why don't you admit it? You're totally jealous of me."

283

Nick flipped the pages of a picture book before placing it in the box next to him. There was a long silence before he answered. "Okay. Maybe I am. But mostly I'm really upset that you're leaving me behind," he said. Dahlia felt a beat of sympathy. Until Nick added, "Leaving our relationship behind—just the way my old girlfriend did."

"Allison?" Dahlia said. She felt an ember of anger ignite. She hadn't thought about Nick's old girlfriend in a long, long time. She hadn't thought there was any reason to. Allison had gone off to college and was just too caught up in her new life to bother keeping in touch. From everything Dahlia had heard about her, Allison was beautiful, exciting—and thoroughly selfish.

Dahlia shook her head in irritation. "Nick, don't you think it's pretty unfair to judge me by the way someone else has behaved?"

Nick raised his shoulders. "It hurt really bad."

"You know, I was never planning on going away and just forgetting about you." Dahlia couldn't even imagine doing that if she wanted to. "You think I'm going to find a new toy and just throw away the old one, is that it? The spoiled rich girl?"

"I didn't say that." Nick frowned. "It's just . . ."

"Just what?"

"Well, you have to admit that you have more than most people."

"If you mean like clothes and CDs and stuff, well, okay. But I don't see what that has to do with anything."

"That stuff—and more. You've traveled all over the world, you have lots of good friends. . . . And we have something pretty great going. At least, we did. But you need this trip abroad, too."

Dahlia felt her frustration growing. "Nick, you've as much as come right out and said that if you were me, you'd go, too."

Nick laughed. "I guess I'd go. Yeah, of course I would. Who am I fooling?" He reached out and touched Dahlia's hand. "It's a great opportunity. I can understand why you want to do it."

Dahlia felt a tingle of pleasure where Nick's hand met hers. They'd been so careful to avoid any contact lately, skirting each other like trains on opposite tracks. She turned her palm up and closed her fingers around his, holding his hand tightly. She could feel the silent love and passion in their simple gesture.

"Maybe I could come visit you over spring break," Nick said softly. "It's going to be hard without you."

Dahlia swallowed. "It's going to be hard without you, too." *And without everyone in Madison. Without Paul and Maya and Matt and Julie . . .* She felt a tug of responsibility. Julie. When she got back here, she was going to need her friends as much as she ever had.

"You know, it's not too late to change my mind," Dahlia said, with a note of reticence.

She could see Nick trying not to smile. "Didn't you send in your acceptance yet?"

Dahlia gave a little laugh. "Maybe they'll apply it to next year." Suddenly, the solution seemed so simple. "Yeah, I could go next year. We could. Maybe we both could. We could both try again. Maybe for our junior year abroad. Rome's not going anywhere. Besides, I've been there three times already. Okay—spoiled— don't say it!"

Nick didn't hold back the smile any longer. He gave her hand a squeeze. "Really?"

"Maybe. I guess it's just not the right time to go." She drew close to Nick to give him a kiss.

But in the second before their lips met, he pulled back abruptly, a worried look stealing across his face. "But if you stay, what are you going to do about your folks?"

Them. Always popping up at the most inconvenient times. "I don't know," Dahlia said slowly. "I guess I'm not going to be able to hide the truth from them much longer. And then—" She made a cutting motion across her neck. "Well, not my neck, actually. My wallet." She sighed. "Maybe I'm going to have to get a job. I guess it's not going to kill me. Or maybe my parents are bluffing."

Nick cupped her face in his hands. "Hey, I have an idea," he said.

"You do?"

He nodded. "Let's not worry about it right now. We'll cross that bridge when we get to it. Together."

Together. Their mouths met in a soft, sexy kiss. And another. And another . . .

Twenty-seven

Home. Seated behind Matt on his motorcycle, her arms wrapped tightly around his waist, Julie thought about what lay ahead. It wasn't going to be easy. Julie knew that as soon as she got back to Madison, she was going to go out to the cemetery and visit Danielle's grave. The memories of her daughter were part of her life now, and there were more tears to be cried.

But the world hadn't stopped. The wind felt good against her face. The air was bracing. Each breath made Julie's whole body tingle. It had been a long time—too long—since she'd written about the Madison town pooper-scooper laws or the new police car, or the fight over granting the Black Angus restaurant a liquor license. She found herself laughing, the sound echoing inside her motorcycle helmet. Yes, she was ready to go back. Ready and eager. She missed school, and all her friends. She had a lot of catching up to do.

Was this the way Matt had felt when he'd won his fight against cancer? That the world was his again? That he was alive again? Having her arms around Matt once again made Julie feel like the luckiest person in the world.

How could she have turned her back on him? Gone from empty to even emptier? She hugged Matt hard. She and Matt had a whole future together. On either side of them, the trees seemed to rush backward, and the road had begun to rise and dip in dramatic hills.

Julie suddenly took notice. This wasn't the familiar route back to Madison! She'd been so lost in thought, she hadn't even been aware that Matt had turned off the main highway. She lifted her helmet visor.

"Matt, I thought you were taking me home!" she yelled into the wind, her breath coming out in a puff of steam.

Matt raised his visor and laughed. "I am."

"This way?"

"A little surprise detour."

"Yeah? Where to?"

Matt just shook his head and put his visor

down, signaling the end of the conversation.

"Matt!" Julie protested, but not very strongly. The truth was, this was one of the things she loved about Matt—the way he'd just whisk her off on some adventure. She felt a heady rush of freedom, something she hadn't come close to feeling since Danielle had died. She put her visor down to protect her face from the cold wind and snuggled up to Matt to enjoy the ride. She tightened her grip on him as he rounded a sharp turn and the bike leaned into the road.

The sound of rushing water under a thin sheet of ice rose from the river next to the road. The hills grew steeper, snaking waterfalls racing down the mountainside into the river. It looked familiar. Someplace Julie felt as if she had been. Someplace special.

Of course! She pushed her helmet visor up. "Riverville!" she announced triumphantly. "We're going back to where we got married! Oh, Matt, you're a hopeless romantic, you know that?"

Soon Matt was slowing down as they passed a sign that announced WELCOME TO RIVERVILLE, ESTABLISHED 1894. Julie recognized the little white church with its tall, wooden spire, the row of neatly kept shops, and then the colonial-style town hall where she and Matt had exchanged their vows.

Matt pulled up in front of the building. A babbling brook ran alongside it. Julie swung her leg over the motorcycle and got off. Matt did, too, pushing down the kickstand with his foot. He took off his helmet and put it down on the ground next to him. Then he removed his leather gloves.

"You, too," he said.

"But, Matt, it's freezing!"

"Jules, you have to!"

Julie laughed, shooting Matt a quizzical expression. "Well . . . okay, but only for a second." She pulled off her purple knit gloves.

Matt held out the hand with his triple wedding bands. "Past, present, and future," he said solemnly.

Julie pressed her own ringed hand into his. "Past, present, future." They drew together in a long, deep kiss. Matt's mouth was soft, searching. Julie felt a swell of love for him. But despite the warmth of their kiss, she shivered as an icy breeze blew up off the brook.

"Matt, I love you, but I'm freezing."

Matt rubbed her hands in his. "Mmm, me, too, and it's still another, what—four, five hours to Madison?"

Julie nodded, her teeth beginning to chatter. "You think there's somewhere we can warm up?" Even as she was asking the question, an idea was occurring to her.

She and Matt looked at each other. He grinned. "The cabin," they both said simultaneously.

It was just as sweet as Julie remembered it. A tiny log cabin—one of about a half-dozen—with a rickety porch, at the edge of a small lake. The lake looked a bit different than it had after the wedding ceremony. Then, the trees around it had been aflame with fall leaves, their colors reflected in the lake's surface. Now, bare trees shared the landscape with evergreens, and the water reflected the silvery play of light and shadow from the cloud-flecked sky above.

As soon as they'd checked in at the little office and had the key, Julie raced up the steps to the front porch of their cabin, just as she had before. As before, Matt was right behind her. He scooped her into his arms, pushed open the door, and carried her over the threshold. He let her down gently.

"My bride," he whispered. He kissed her cheek. She felt the tender warmth of his lips on her cold skin.

"My groom." She kissed him back, soft, light kisses on his cheek and brow.

They drew apart and shrugged out of their

jackets. Julie sat down on the edge of the bed and unlaced her boots. She wriggled her feet out of them, lay back on the bed, her head propped up on pillows, and massaged her toes back to life. Matt knelt down in front of the fireplace, removed the grate, and began building a fire. Julie glanced around the room. Done all in wood and shades of green, she remembered thinking last time how it was like a forest lair. Deep-green curtains, grass-green rug, pine dresser with two dark oak easy chairs. The bedspread was lake blue.

As the fire caught, the room was filled with the comforting smell that rides the air on cold nights. The fire crackled. Julie watched Matt wipe his hands on his jeans and come over to lie down next to her.

He slung his arm around her shoulders. "Wow, is it really only a little over a year since we were here? I mean, the place feels the same—familiar, kind of like it's ours. But I feel like so much has happened . . ." He kissed her softly on the mouth. "Remember how hard it was in the beginning? And then my illness . . . And then—" He left the rest of the thought hanging.

"Danielle," Julie finished quietly, a lump forming in her throat.

Matt folded her in a bear hug. They lay

silent for a long time, watching the flame lick the logs and listening to the fire spit and crackle. Julie was keenly aware of the feeling of Matt's arms around her, his body with hers.

"There's one good thing, Julie," Matt murmured, his lips brushing her cheek.

"Mm?" Julie snuggled closer.

"You *know* after everything we've been through, we're going to be there for each other—always. Through thick and thin."

Julie felt the warmth of Matt's words spread through her whole body. It felt so wonderful to have someone love her this much.

"And know what else?" he asked.

"What else?" Julie saw that Matt's deep-set gray eyes were sparkling.

"It's going to be an adventure. New experiences, new places . . . Speaking of which, I remember lying here last time and promising you a real honeymoon," Matt said. "The Mediterranean, I think it was. When are we going to do it?"

Julie brought his hand to her mouth and kissed it. "The night we had here was honeymoon enough for me, Matt."

Matt laughed. "Well, maybe sometime soon we'll go on another one, somewhere we've never been before. Mexico or California, or someplace we've never even heard of."

"Maybe," Julie said. "I've got a lot of work to do when we get back, but maybe over winter break. When a little more time has passed." More time. More healing. She thought about holding Danielle that one and only time. The feel of her soft, soft skin, the tiny fingers and toes. A tear formed in the corner of her eye. But for the first time, she knew she *would* heal, knew she would be ready for the long, adventurous road that lay ahead for her and Matt.

Matt cupped her face and turned it toward his. He kissed the tear away—lingeringly, gently. "Julie," he whispered. He kissed her brow, her nose, her mouth. His lips were warm on her lips.

Julie felt herself relaxing into the moment. She stroked the side of Matt's face, slightly rough from not shaving. Their kisses deepened. He rubbed his hand up and down her back. She ran her fingers through his thick hair. She slid her hand under his T-shirt and traced the swell of lean muscles. He kissed the curve of her neck, his lips finding an extra-sensitive spot. They pressed closer, closer.

They undressed each other, punctuating every movement with kisses and caresses.

They explored each other as if it were the first time. They made love slowly, all sense of time lost to their passion.

"I love you, Julie," Matt whispered.

"I love you, Matt. Forever," she whispered back.

"Forever," he answered.